INSINCERE PRAISE FOR I HAVE A BAD FEELING ABOUT THIS

"*I Have a Bad Feeling About This* is more fun than a barrel of monkeys! Of course, when you think about it, a barrel of monkeys isn't that much fun. It's kind of sad really. Look at them all crammed in there. Poor monkeys." —*The Los Angeles Snob Report*

"Better than *To Kill a Mockingbird*, *Catcher in the Rye*, and *Fahrenheit 451* combined! But not as good as *Animal Farm*, *Lord of the Flies*, and *The Adventures of Huckleberry Finn* combined. Better than *Pride and Prejudice* but not as good as the version of *Pride and Prejudice* where they added zombies." —*The London Babbler*

"I read this entire book in one sitting! Sure, it was a long sitting, maybe seventeen or eighteen hours, and I took some breaks to watch TV and eat some ranch-flavored potato chips, but I did remain sitting the whole time. I guess I'm just one lazy, lazy human being. I feel such shame. Such deep, deep shame. But hey, what are you gonna do? Pass me some more chips, will ya?" —*New York Goober*

"One star out of five. This book is so dumb i want 2 punch the dumb writer of this dumb book LOL if i ever meet the writer im going 2 be all like, *hey, why are u so dumb?* and when he says somethin dumb im going 2 punch him LOL." —Bob in Detroit (via Amazon)

"It was okay, I guess, if you're into this kind of stuff." —Jeff Strand, author of *A Bad Day for Voodoo*

I HAVE A BAD FEELING ABOUT THIS

JEFF STRAND

sourcebooks
fire

Published by Sourcebooks Fire, an imprint of Sourcebooks, Inc.
P.O. Box 4410, Naperville, Illinois 60567-4410
(630) 961-3900
Fax: (630) 961-2168
www.sourcebooks.com

Library of Congress Cataloging-in-Publication Data is on file with the publisher.

Printed and bound in the United States of America.
VP 19 18

"Life is like a box of chocolates. You never know what you're gonna get."
—FORREST GUMP

"Actually, Forrest, boxes of chocolates usually have a guide on the underside of the lid that shows you exactly what you're going to get."
—ANONYMOUS

"If you sprinkle
When you tinkle,
Please be a sweetie
And wipe the seatie."
—WILLIAM SHAKESPEARE

CHAPTER ZERO

"Hi, everybody. This is Rad Rad Roger here at the world premiere of *I Have a Bad Feeling About This*, and let me tell you, this par-taaay is wild! You can't spit without hitting a celebrity! Watch—I'm gonna try it right now. *Hoooccccccchhhhh—patoo*!"

"*Hey*! What the—"

"It's Academy Award nominee Sandy Klifton! Great to see you here! Is that a baby bump?"

"No, it most certainly is not."

"Are you suuuuuure? No, no, I'm just playing around. Celebrities wouldn't lie about something like that. So are you looking forward to the movie?"

"Well, sure, I mean, that's kind of why I'm here."

"Me too, me too. Not that I have tickets. Wanna sell me yours? No, no, I'm just playing around. Who's your baby daddy? C'mon, you can tell me. We'll edit that part out of the live broadcast."

"I have to go now."

"That was Academy Award non-winner Sandy Klifton, off to have some nighttime morning sickness! And I'm Rad Rad Roger with continuing coverage of tonight's festivities! Ooh! Ooh! Home run! It's Henry Lambert! How's it going, Henry?"

"It's going great!"

"So you're a pretty big deal. Sixteen years old and they've made a movie out of your life!"

"Well, I'm not sixteen anymore. I was sixteen when everything happened, but I've aged since then."

"Ooooh, *burn*! Have you seen the movie yet?"

"They let me watch the rough cut, yeah."

"Is it accurate?"

"Well, it's Hollywood. This isn't supposed to be a documentary."

"How accurate is it?"

"It's…uh…"

"You definitely have smaller muscles in real life."

"Yeah, I guess so."

"The commercial shows you running away from an explosion with a machine gun in each hand. Can I touch your arm? I just want to see if it could really hold a machine gun like that."

"I'd rather you didn't."

"Oh, yeah, no way could this skinny thing hold a machine gun. Not even a small one."

"Excuse me, sir. I'm afraid we're going to have to ask you to leave."

"Hey, I'm Internet sensation Rad Rad Roger! I'll leave when my viewers have gotten the full story on the world premiere of *I Have a Bad Feeling About This*!"

"Sir, you and your crew need to leave immediately. I won't ask again."

"Ladies and gentlemen, this is Rad Rad Roger, bringing you live coverage of me being thrown out of the—okay, okay, ow, stop it! Ow! All I did was touch his arm! *I Have a Bad Feeling About This* is a lie! Ow! Ow! You're scuffing up my suit! If you want the true story of what happened out there, read the book! Read the booooooooook!"

CHAPTER ONE

"Is your son a scrawny little wuss?" asked the man on the YouTube video.

Henry felt like he was getting a sunburn from the eyes glaring at him through the computer. *Wuss? Nerd*, sure. *Geek*, yeah. *Dork*, not since fifth grade. *Not always operating at maximum courage levels*, he could accept. But *wuss* was definitely going too far.

The drill-instructor narrator was bald, dressed in camouflage, and had biceps as big as a standard-sized human head. The camera zoomed in on his face and Henry could see the vein pulsing on his forehead, like he had an angry worm in there. "It doesn't have to be this way!" the narrator said, his voice echoing dramatically. "We can *Fix! Your! Son!*"

On the screen, a line of boys walked through the woods. One of them tripped. Another one walked into a tree branch. A third started frantically slapping at something that had crawled down the back of his shirt. The muscular man stepped into the frame and shook his head.

"Disgraceful, isn't it? It would make me want to cry, except *Men! Don't! Cry!* At least not after they've gone through—"

There was a whoosh and then a loud clank as the following words slammed onto the screen in manly steel letters: STRONGWOODS SURVIVAL CAMP!!! The words exploded.

It was kind of a cheesy explosion. Henry could have done a much better one on his own computer. Unfortunately, he didn't think that his dad was making him watch this video to get his opinion on the quality of the special effects.

"Two weeks at Strongwoods Survival Camp is all it takes to turn your cowardly lion into a fearless panther! He will learn how to stand up for himself…and how to survive! Whether it's school or the zombie apocalypse, our graduates fear nothing!"

A small caption read *"Disclaimer: Zombie apocalypses are fictional and not part of the Strongwoods Survival Camp curriculum."*

"We teach archery!" A shot of an arrow hitting a bull's-eye.

"Hand-to-hand combat!" A kid punched a bigger kid in the face, apparently knocking him unconscious with one blow.

"Water transport!" A fearless kid rode a canoe through violent rapids.

"Hunting!" A kid strangled a deer, though a caption read *"Re-enactment. Do not attempt."*

"And more! More! More!" The camera zoomed way too close to his face. "Strongwoods Survival Camp!" the man shouted, getting a bit of saliva on the camera lens. "Register your scrawny wimp of a son today!"

Henry's dad turned to face him. "So what do you think?"

Henry stared at the screen for several seconds before he spoke. "This is a joke, right?"

"No, it's real, and we think it would be good for you."

"See, I was kind of thinking the exact opposite. Literally. The exact opposite. One hundred and eighty degrees."

"You mean three-sixty."

Henry shook his head. "One-eighty. Three-sixty brings you back to where you started."

"Oh, you're right."

"Maybe you need geometry camp."

"Maybe you need to stop being a wise guy. Your mother and I just want what's best for you. This could be a life-changing experience."

"More like a life-ending experience."

"This could turn you into a man. How were you planning to become a man?"

"I just kind of thought my body would keep growing."

"Henry, you're a good kid. You're smart, your grades are fantastic, and we're proud of you, but there are gaps in your life skills. This will help fill some of them."

"I'm sixteen," said Henry. "I'm way too old for summer camp. That's for little kids."

"This isn't summer camp. This is survival camp. Your mother and I don't expect you to become captain of the football team or even demonstrate mild competence at bowling, but wouldn't it be nice if bullies didn't kick sand in your face?"

"Nobody has ever actually kicked sand in my face."

"And do you know why? Because you never go to the beach. And do you know why you never go to the beach? Because you're afraid of sharks."

"So? That's a good fear! It keeps me from getting eaten!"

"But it's not just sharks. You're scared of jellyfish—"

"Which sting you!"

"Barracuda—"

"Monsters from hell."

"Lobsters—"

"Well, duh."

"Seahorses—"

"I'm not proud of that."

Okay, Henry did have a fairly long list of fears, but still…*wuss* was too harsh. It wasn't like he slept with a night light or peeked under the bed for tentacled monsters. He just had a healthy fear of nature's vicious predators. And seahorses.

"Halibut—"

"I never said I was scared of halibut. I said that the way they've got both eyes on the same side of their face was creepy. I didn't want to swim directly into one. What's wrong with that?"

His dad sighed. "The thing is...you could overcome these fears."

"Going out in the woods is going to conquer my fear of jellyfish?"

His father sighed. "Look, Henry, I can't force you to go. Actually, I can. That's the whole point. If you went to this camp, then nobody could force you to go to camp ever again. Don't you want strength? Don't you want self-confidence?"

Actually, Henry wanted both of those things. Though he would never, ever, ever admit this to anybody, he was always envious of the guys who could easily talk to girls or who could play team sports without embarrassing and/or hurting themselves. Not that he wanted to be a jock or anything—that would be ridiculous. Still, he was pretty sure that girls would like him once they got to know him. It would be nice to have the self-confidence to say, "Hi, I'm Henry. Wanna get to know me?" (He wouldn't say it in quite that manner of course. That was just the general concept of what he'd say if he had self-confidence.)

But he didn't want to acquire those skills at a camp with that guy in the video bellowing at him for two weeks. Henry was short, skinny, and nerdy/geeky—the ultimate prey for a noisy bodybuilder.

"Are you sure Mom wants me to go?"

"Yes."

"Then why are we talking about it when she's in Delaware for the week?"

"Your mother may not be quite as sold on the idea as I am, but she definitely agrees with the general concept…in theory."

"Do I still have to scoop ice cream when I get back?"

"Yes. Anyway, I'll give you some time to think about it, but you should go with Randy."

"Wait a minute—Randy's going?"

* * *

"It's gonna be the greatest thing ever!" Randy shouted, forcing Henry to hold the phone a couple of feet away from his ear. "Two weeks of awesome sauce!"

"It looks like two weeks of torture sauce," Henry said. They'd been best friends since kindergarten and Henry was used to Randy being extremely enthusiastic about things, but these things were usually related to Facebook posts rather than physical exertion. Randy got out of breath if he ate corn on the cob too quickly.

"Are you kidding me? Did you even look at the website? There are going to be survival games just like *The Hunger Games* in real life!"

"Seriously?"

"Yeah!"

"Well, that might be kind of cool," Henry admitted.

"This'll be the best summer of our lives."

"You understand that there won't be any girls there, right?"

"So?" Randy asked. "What difference does it make if there are zero girls at survival camp or eight hundred girls here that we don't talk to?"

"Good point. Good, depressing point."

"Anyway, there is an all-girl camp somewhere around there, although I think it's more about music and less about violence."

"Well, that's encouraging," said Henry. "Maybe we can get more dates if we ask at crossbow point. So we're really going to do this, huh?"

"I don't know about you, but I am."

"All right, all right. Then I guess I am too. But I have a bad fee—"

"Sorry, gotta go. Talk to you tomorrow."

* * *

"Do you realize it's two thirty in the morning?" Henry's dad asked, walking into the living room, fastening his bathrobe.

Henry kept his attention on the TV screen. "Yeah."

"Have you considered going to bed?"

"It's going to be two weeks without video games. I have to play enough now to sustain myself through that time."

"That game actually looks kind of cool."

"It is. And it's helping me build my survival skills before camp."

In this game, mummies had taken over the world, and the player's job was to kill them. It was kind of astonishing how many ways there were to kill a mummy. Though Henry could safely say that there would not be any mummy-killing exercises at camp, the dexterity and problem-solving skills he was demonstrating now would help him in real life, right?

"All right. Whatever. Have fun."

WILDERNESS SURVIVAL TIP!

Ninety-seven percent of our nation's ponds are filled to the top with piranha, which can skeletonize a cow in seconds. If you value your cow, don't shove it into a pond.

CHAPTER TWO

Henry didn't much like the outdoors and there was a *lot* of outdoors out here. Randy sat next to him in the backseat of the car, looking giddy. He was too old to say, "Are we there yet? Are we there yet? Are we there yet?" but Henry could tell that he was saying it in his mind. Randy had talked about nothing but Strongwoods Survival Camp for the past ten days, and Henry had to admit that his enthusiasm was infectious. It might be kind of cool. It might even be fun. He might even put in a solid twenty-third-place showing in the Games, assuming that there were twenty-six or twenty-seven other players.

Henry still didn't like the outdoors, though.

They'd been on a dirt road for the past fifteen miles. The car made a *THUB THUB THUB* sound, and Henry kept glancing out the rear window to make sure that useful pieces weren't being left behind. After the road had degenerated to the point where you could no longer accurately refer to it as a road, they reached a sign that said, "Welcome to Strongwoods Survival Camp."

"I think that sign is written in blood," said Henry.

"Oh, it is not," said his mother.

"Randy, doesn't that look like blood?"

Randy shook his head. "It's too bright. Blood's brown when it dries."

The woods seemed to suddenly get darker and spookier. This place could be the hunting grounds for at least seven or eight different serial killers. Coming here was such a bad idea. Henry was going to look like a total idiot when he wound up dismembered.

"Oh, well," the chief of police would say, "that's what you get for ignoring a sign written in blood."

Finally, they reached the camp. It consisted of two small buildings, both of them brown and nondescript. The one that was slightly less nondescript had a black truck parked in front of it. There was also a flagpole that didn't look like it could support the weight of an actual flag.

Henry's dad shut off the car. As they got out, the front door to one of the brown buildings opened, and the bald, muscular man from the video walked out. He was wearing the same camouflage outfit, unless he owned more than one.

"Welcome to Strongwoods Survival Camp," he said. "My name is Max." He looked at Henry. "You must be Randy Cakes."

"I'm Henry Lambert. He's Randy."

Henry suddenly wondered if he'd made a terrible mistake by correcting the man. Maybe he and Randy should have just switched identities for the next two weeks.

But Max smiled. "Good to meet both of you. We discourage long good-byes here—they make you weak—so if you boys want to take your stuff into the barracks, we'll send your parents on their way."

Henry's dad popped open the lid of the trunk and Henry and Randy each took out their backpacks and duffel bags. Max had a sour expression on his face as Henry received a hug from his mom and Henry suspected that if a crowbar had been lying around, Max would have used it to pry them apart.

"Say good-bye to the old Henry and Randy," Max said.

"The next time you see these fine young men, you'll barely recognize them."

Henry didn't like the sound of that. It *could* mean that they'd leave survival camp with a bold new attitude, but it could also mean that his face was about to be grotesquely disfigured.

Henry's dad shook his hand, hopefully not for the last time, and then his parents got back into the car and drove away. Soon, they were far enough away that even if Henry *wanted* to run after them, waving his arms and screaming "Don't leeeeeeeave me heeeeeeeere!" he couldn't catch up.

Max pointed to the second brown building. "Take your stuff in there and pick a cot."

Henry and Randy nodded and went into the building. Inside, there were about twenty non-comfy-looking cots, ten against each wall. Only three of them appeared to have been claimed so far by three boys who all looked up as they entered.

"Hi!" said Randy.

Henry was immediately relieved to see that two of the three boys were unimpressive physical specimens like himself. In fact, one of them, a kid with short spiky hair that was dyed green, was only about thirteen. The other one was tall and gawky, with limbs that looked easily snappable. The third kid—and the only one who seemed remotely athletic—was probably a year older than Henry. He had the lean, muscular physique of the kids on the swim team and looked like he spent as much time on his hair as Henry spent helping Mario save the princess.

"Are we that early?" asked Henry, tossing his stuff on the nearest cot. They were supposed to be here by noon and it was only a few minutes before that.

The tall/gawky kid shook his head. "Nah. It's just the five of us."

"Are you kidding me?"

"Nope."

Only five people? You couldn't hide in the background if there were only five people! Five people meant plenty of individual attention! Twenty percent of Max's focus would be on him! He was doomed.

Henry wanted to vomit right onto his new cot, but he thought the others might take that as a sign of weakness.

The door opened and Max entered the barracks, scowling. "Everybody line up!" he shouted.

The five of them lined up.

"As you know, my name is Max, but if you call me Max, I'll pop your head like a ripe zit. During your time here, I am *sir*. Got it?"

"Yes, sir!" said Randy.

"Everybody!"

"Yes, sir!" said everybody. Henry was glad that it was the green-haired kid and not him who was a beat behind.

"The instructions clearly said that you were to bring no cell phones or other portable electronic devices to camp. But somebody *always* brings a cell phone or other portable electronic device to camp. Every single time. Now I am going to offer you an extremely brief grace period in which you can hand over this contraband because if I discover it, it will not merely be confiscated. It will be *destroyed*. Ten…nine…eight—"

Henry rushed over to his cot and hurriedly unzipped his duffel bag. The other four boys did the same. Henry removed his cell phone from the hidden pocket, his iPod from another hidden pocket, and his portable gaming device from the pocket of a folded-up shirt.

After he had collected five cell phones, four iPods, six gaming devices, and a laptop computer, Max lined the boys back up again. "Thank you for your cooperation. Now everybody pour the contents of your bags onto your cots."

They each went to their cots and emptied out their bags. Henry wanted to debate the constitutionality of this search, but he also didn't want to get on Max's radar any more than absolutely necessary.

Max went over to the green-haired kid's cot and looked at his things. He picked up a pair of socks that was folded into a ball.

"Jackie!"

"Yes, sir?"

"Why are these socks heavier than I would expect a ball of socks this size to be?"

"They're thick socks, sir."

"If I unfold these socks, will I discover more than just sock?"

"No, sir. The socks are also dirty, which might account for the added weight, sir."

"You brought dirty socks?"

"Yes, sir. I waited until the last minute to pack and didn't realize I didn't have any clean socks, sir. And I get rocks in my shoes sometimes, which might have gotten into my socks, which could also explain why they're so heavy, sir."

"Since these are socks, only socks, and nothing but socks, would you mind if I threw them on the floor and stomped on them?"

"I'd rather you didn't, sir."

Max handed the socks to Jackie. "Unfold them."

"This is kind of unsanitary, sir."

"Do it."

Jackie's shoulders slumped as he unfolded the socks, revealing an iPhone.

"My, my, my, my, my, my, my, what do we have here?" asked Max.

"Please don't harm it, sir."

"Would you mind telling me what you were thinking?"

"Sir, I was thinking that I lack confidence in my social skills and I felt that sneaking in an iPhone would help me bond with my fellow campers, sir."

Max snatched the phone out of his hand. "Well, Jackie, you're in luck because it's against camp policy to destroy private property. But it's not against camp policy to make you do push-ups until you puke. Down on the floor. Now!"

Jackie dropped to the floor and began to do push-ups.

"You think that's funny?" Max asked Randy for no reason that Henry could explain since Randy's mouth had been completely horizontal the entire time.

"No, sir."

"You want to get down there with him?"

"No, sir."

"On the floor, Randy! Show me what you've got!"

Randy hesitated.

"I said…on the floor!"

"He can't make you do that," Henry said. "This isn't the military."

The words were out before Henry realized what he was saying. *This* was when he decided to have a surprising moment of courage? Seriously?

As Max stepped in front of Henry and fixed his steel-eyed gaze upon him, Henry knew that the next two weeks of his life were going to really, truly suck.

WILDERNESS SURVIVAL TIP!

An empty shampoo bottle can be used to make about one-eightieth of a raft. So when you go hiking, be sure to bring eighty empty shampoo bottles.

CHAPTER THREE

"What did you say?" asked Max.

"Nothing." Henry desperately tried to think of something that rhymed with "He can't make you do that. This isn't the military" so that he could pretend he'd said that instead, but nothing came to mind.

"No, no, please, satisfy my curiosity. What did you say to your buddy?"

"All I said was that, you know, we're not in the army. This is survival camp. We're paying you, right? To teach us skills and stuff? So the drill sergeant thing is fun and all—I'm not saying you should quit doing it—but you can't really force us to do push-ups until we puke."

Max's gaze did not waver. Henry suspected that the thought process going through his mind was *not* "Gosh, perhaps this youngster is right."

"Tell me, son," said Max, "how far away are we from the rest of civilization right now?"

"Very."

"So what makes you think I won't just kill you where you stand?"

"Well…I mean…we all know that you're not actually going to *kill* me, right? I have a lot of dumb fears—you can ask anybody—and I'm not trying to say that you *couldn't* kill me if you tried. I'm sure you could. But it would never occur to me to worry that you were going to take an actual human life. That doesn't make any sense, not when you're trying to run a business. I totally understand that you were exaggerating, but even if you just threatened to beat me up, you wouldn't do that. You'd lose your license, right?"

Henry was sort of impressed by his own bravery. He was a completely new person. Maybe survival camp had done its job already and he could go home.

He glanced over at Randy, who didn't look like he agreed that there wouldn't be a murder today.

Max cracked his knuckles. Each crack sounded like a cannon going off. Henry suddenly felt significantly less courageous.

Crap! He was going to freaking die. Why didn't real life have a restore function so he could take back the last thirty seconds?

"I'm sorry," Henry said.

"No, no, don't apologize," said Max. "You're right. I can't kill you or hit you. All I can do is make your accommodations less comfortable. That's all. Nothing more. Less comfortable accommodations."

"Really, I'm sorry. I don't know what happened. I think your testosterone level is contagious."

"Less comfortable accommodations," Max repeated. "Not a big deal. You'll barely notice the difference. It's not something to worry about. Please don't let your stress over what I mean by 'less comfortable accommodations' ruin such a lovely day."

Henry felt sick to his stomach. He definitely preferred the noisy Max to the sinister one.

"I'm really—"

"Do not apologize again. Apologies are for the weak. When the power finally goes out for good and the looters have broken through your front door and you're out of bullets, saying you're sorry is a good way to get a machete in the face. Jackie, you may stand back up now."

Jackie, who had only done half a push-up, stood up and returned to his place in line. Max picked up Jackie's sock, dropped it onto the wooden floor, and then stomped on it several times with his heavy boots. Jackie let out a progressively more pained whimper with each stomp. *Wham! Eep! Wham! Eeep! Wham! Eeeep! Wham! Eeeeep!*

Max picked up the sock and shook the iPhone pieces out onto Jackie's cot. Then he folded his arms over his chest. "Here's what you wormy maggoty slugs need to understand: I have to reimburse Jackie for that stupid phone now. I knew that while I was breaking it and I have a very limited income. But I don't care. Those few seconds of destruction were worth it to me. And I may just decide that the crunch of a bone is worth having your parents file a lawsuit. So when I tell you to do something, you do it! Do you understand?"

"Yes, sir!" said everybody, especially including Henry.

"Do not expect luxury during your stay. The showers *will* be cold. The food *will* be disgusting. There is only one thing in the entire world that I truly fear, and that is the outhouse you will be using. Don't expect to find the bunny-soft, fluffy toilet paper that you get at home; this stuff *hurts*. Are there any questions?"

"No, sir!" said the boys.

"Good! Now I will give you two minutes—that is one hundred and twenty seconds, exactly half of four minutes—to finish getting yourselves settled in. When you hear the bell, report to the other building for lunch. Got it?"

"Yes, sir!"

"But first, Henry, drop to the floor and give me push-ups until you puke."

It only took nine.

* * *

"This isn't so bad," said Randy, chewing on a carrot that had the texture of a gummy worm.

"Yeah," said Jackie, taking a bite of his crunchy bologna sandwich. "From the way he was talking, I thought it would be a lot worse."

The tall and gawky kid, Stu, took a drink. Nobody could quite tell if it was regular milk or chocolate milk, but the general consensus was that it was probably milk. "I've had worse."

Erik poked at his cherry cobbler. It had been sizzling when it was put on his tray five minutes ago and it hadn't stopped yet. The tip of his fork was starting to melt, but it was plastic, not metal, so they weren't too concerned.

Henry had not yet worked up the nerve or the appetite to unwrap the three foil-covered items on his plate. Strongwoods Survival Camp did not have a chef. Max had made their lunch, though he explained that they would be dividing up those duties for future meals. The other four boys had gone down the line with their trays and received their food, but Max had calmly said, "Here's something special for you," when it was Henry's turn.

"Just open them," Randy urged.

"Do it," said Erik. "It's not like he's going to poison you. If he wanted to kill you, he'd just rip your neck open."

Henry sighed. One of the items was vaguely circular. One was vaguely cylindrical and the other might have been a foil-wrapped starfish. Fortunately, none of them were moving.

"You'll be sorry if you don't," said Jackie. "You barfed up all your nutrition."

"I'm not hungry."

"What you should do is you think of all the most horrible things they could be and then when you open them, they won't seem so bad."

"Okay," said Randy, playing along. "That long one could be a tongue with hair on it."

"Do you really think that helps?" asked Henry.

"Unwrap it."

Henry pulled away enough of the foil to reveal that whatever was inside had at least one eye. He closed the foil and pushed back his chair. "I'm done."

"What was it?" asked Stu.

"You can have it."

"Thanks." Stu picked up the object and unwrapped the foil. "It's a fish head, like in that song about fish heads. Here, catch." He tossed it to Henry, who missed on purpose but probably would have missed on accident too. The fish head landed on the floor, and an alarming number of ants were swarming on it before Henry could blink.

Stu grabbed the other two items off Henry's plate. "Let's see what the other ones are." He unwrapped the star-shaped one. Each point contained a dead beetle and the middle contained a bigger dead beetle.

"That's pretty gross," said Stu. "Though not as gross as the head. We should have opened the beetles first so there was an escalation in grossness."

Henry shrugged. "I'm kind of disappointed, to tell the truth. Beetles? Really? He thinks he's going to break my spirit by serving me beetles for lunch? I watch *Survivor* every week. Dead beetles aren't going to freak me out. I'm honestly offended by that. Max acts like he's so big and tough, but this is something that I'd expect from a third-grader. What did he think I was going to do? Run out of here screaming? 'Ew! Ew! Beetles! Poor me!' If you want to know the truth, the guy is pathetic. Flat-out pathetic. If he was here, I'd laugh right in his big ugly face." Henry paused. "He's behind me, isn't he?"

"Nope," said Randy. "He's still in the back."

"Thank God. So anyway, like I was saying…beetles? That's weak. I think he's all talk."

"He smashed my phone," said Jackie.

"I think he's all talk except for that one time when he smashed your phone."

The back door opened. Max walked into the room and over to their table. "Your lunch is on the floor," he said to Henry.

"I wasn't hungry," Henry informed him.

"In a survival situation, you maximize your food resources. If you were trapped on a desert island, starving to death, ribs about to pop through your skin, do you think you would throw a perfectly good fish head on the floor?"

"The head isn't edible."

"Is that so?"

"I don't really know," Henry admitted. "Literally zero percent of my life has been spent researching that."

Max glared at him. "*Sir.*"

"I don't really know. Literally zero percent of my life has been spent researching that, *sir.*"

"You can boil a fish head and make a perfectly fine soup. Or you can use it to attract ants, which as we all know are a good source of protein. Was your intention to attract ants to use as a good source of protein?"

"No, sir." Henry was not opposed to telling a lie, but he thought it was best if he didn't tell a completely transparent one.

"Beetles are also a good source of protein. In a survival situation, the man who eats beetles lives and the man who says that they're icky dies. If you were lying in the middle of the forest, both legs broken, vocal cords shredded from screams that nobody answered, seconds away from death via starvation, are you telling me you wouldn't eat a beetle?"

"Under those circumstances, I would gobble down beetles left and right," Henry said.

Max plucked one of the beetles out of the tinfoil and popped it into his mouth. He chewed noisily. "Does that disgust you?" he asked.

"No, I mean, it's not something I'd watch on purpose, but I've seen way worse on TV. I've seen people eat baby turtles."

"Baby turtles?"

"Yeah."

Max frowned. "That's not right."

"I'll eat a beetle," said Jackie. He popped one into his mouth and smiled happily as he chewed. He swallowed and then ate the remaining two small ones. "Steamed perfectly. Thank you, sir."

Max pointed at Henry, getting his index finger a sixteenth of an inch from Henry's nose. "I am not impressed with you so far. Not at all. You need to step up your game if you want to make it through these next two weeks. And I hope you realize that I'm just trying to make you into a better, stronger person, and I'm not a complete monster." He tapped the last remaining foil-covered item on Henry's plate. "Now, eat your hot dog so we can start our first training session."

WILDERNESS SURVIVAL TIP!

Bear cubs may look all fluffy and fuzzy and adorable and snuggly, but if you try to hug them, you'll discover that deep inside, they're total jerks.

CHAPTER FOUR

"Weapons," said Max. "Weapons are a good thing. As satisfying as it is to kill something with your bare hands, that's not always practical."

The five boys stood outside in a clearing. On the other side of the clearing, about a hundred feet away, five paper targets were mounted on bales of hay. Max, now wearing a heavy black vest, paced in front of them.

"In a survival situation, you may find yourself encountering an individual who wishes to do you harm. That individual may be a puma operating on pure instinct or a human operating on pure evil. The one thing these two individuals have in common is that they both do poorly against a grenade."

Max reached inside his vest pocket and pulled out a grenade. All five boys took a great big step back.

"A hand grenade, though deadly to your enemies, is perfectly safe to you as long as you remember to throw it. Forgetting to throw a grenade is one dumb way to lose an arm."

He pulled out the pin and just stood there.

"Ummmm—" said three out of the five boys.

Max continued to stand there.

Was he really going to blow off his arm just to make an educational point?

After about ten seconds, Max tucked the grenade back into his vest. "Had that been a real grenade, you would have all been hit by bone fragments. Getting hit in the eye by a shard of arm bone because you were too stupid to move out of the way is one of the least intelligent ways that you can go blind. So in the future, when you see a presumably deranged man standing there holding a live grenade, you *duck and cover*!"

"Yes, sir!" said Randy.

"Let's try that again." Max reached back into his vest and pulled out the grenade.

The boys dove to the ground. Henry put his hands over his eyes and cringed as he waited for the explosion.

He waited some more. No explosion yet.

The next few moments of waiting were also explosion-free.

After another few moments, Henry began to suspect that there would not be an explosion.

"Everybody on your feet," said Max.

Henry and the others got back up.

"In a survival situation, it is important to use the information that has been provided to you. If you know that your enemy is holding a fake grenade, don't drop to the ground and act like it's going to blow up. That's just ignorant."

"Sir," said Erik, "how can we *trust* you when you say it's a fake grenade? Our enemy could be making up stories about phony grenades so that we'll lower our defenses." He smiled a bit at his own cleverness.

"Excellent point. What if it is a real grenade and I just hadn't released the lever?"

Max released the lever, which popped off the grenade and landed on the ground.

Erik screamed.

Randy screamed.

Jackie screamed.

Stu screamed.

Henry fainted.

*　*　*

Henry opened his eyes. All he saw was dirt. He rolled over. Randy was crouched over him, looking concerned.

"How long was I out?"

"Three days," said Randy.

"For real?"

"No, more like thirty seconds."

Henry sat up. Max, who still had all his limbs and facial features, did not look impressed with him. Henry brushed the dirt off his shirt, thinking that preserving his dignity might be a challenge.

He'd never fainted before. To be honest, he hadn't even thought that people really *did* faint from fear; he'd always just sort of assumed that it was something that happened in the movies but not real life, like talking to yourself in the mirror.

"Are you all right?" asked Max.

"Yeah, I'm fine."

"You're sure? Not feeling all swoony like you've just seen Justin Beeder?"

"Justin Bieber," Henry said.

"I hope you don't think that you earned more respect by correcting me."

Henry got to his feet. He still felt a little woozy but forced himself to remain upright.

"In a survival situation, fainting means death," Max told everybody. "Do you think that if you fainted in front of the

Nazis, they'd give you smelling salts and wait for you to recover? One of the simplest rules of self-defense is that it's easier to keep your enemies at bay when you are conscious. Do you understand, Henry?"

"Yes, sir."

"As I hope you've all noticed, that was not a live grenade. We do have live grenades, carefully locked away, and I will indeed show you how to throw them. But as Fainting Boy has proven, you're not ready yet. Instead, we will be learning archery."

He walked over to a large black bag that rested on the ground, knelt down beside it, and unzipped it. He took out a bow.

Randy almost bounced with excitement.

"How many of you have shot a bow and arrow before?" Max asked.

Erik raised his hand.

"Anybody else? Stu? Jackie? Randy? Swooning Henry?"

Everybody else shook their heads.

Max looked disgusted. "Are you all telling me that you've spent sixteen years on this planet and you haven't ever shot a bow and arrow?"

"I'm only thirteen, sir," said Jackie.

"Then you're excused."

"I've shot arrows before," said Randy, "but they had suction cups on the end. If that counts. I'm guessing it doesn't."

"You know what, Randy?" said Max. "The bar has been set so low that I'll count that."

"Thank you, sir."

Max took several arrows out of the bag, set them on the ground, and then zipped the bag shut again. He picked up one arrow and stood up.

"The arrows we will be using have steel tips. Steel, when shot at a high velocity, will puncture flesh. This means that if you shoot yourself in the foot, you see a lot of blood. Do not shoot yourself in the foot. Do not shoot your fellow campers. If I have to take your bows and arrows away from you due to safety concerns, it will accelerate my spiral into depression and camp life will not be pleasant. Does everybody understand?"

Everybody indicated that they understood.

"Mr. Fainty, before I demonstrate proper technique, I need somebody to demonstrate the incorrect way. So why don't you shoot the first arrow?"

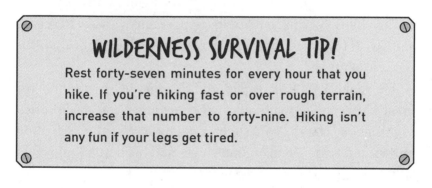

WILDERNESS SURVIVAL TIP!

Rest forty-seven minutes for every hour that you hike. If you're hiking fast or over rough terrain, increase that number to forty-nine. Hiking isn't any fun if your legs get tired.

CHAPTER FIVE

Henry was surprised to discover that he looked forward to being the first one to shoot the arrows. This could be his chance to redeem himself. This could be his opportunity to make Max gasp and say, "Holy frack! This guy can shoot! I'll leave him alone for the rest of camp!"

He could show Erik, Jackie, and Stu that he wasn't the most inept kid in the group. Randy, of course, had too much inside information; Henry could shoot a million arrows into a million targets and score a million bull's-eyes and his best friend would still know that he wasn't truly cool.

And worst-case scenario, he'd miss. So what?

Well, okay, in the worst-case scenario, the bow would slip out of his hands a few times and everybody would have a merry laugh. Then he'd put the arrow in the wrong way, maybe even sideways. Max would yell at him for a few dozen hours. Henry would vow to get it right this time, so he'd carefully notch the arrow, pull it back, take careful aim, and then the string would break. The arrow would go wild and Henry would think *Please don't let it hit anybody, but if it's absolutely necessary that it hit somebody, please don't let it be Randy*, so naturally, the arrow would go right through Randy's head, protruding out the other side, and he'd get that silly expression that people do when an arrow goes through their head.

Randy's brain wouldn't be functioning properly because of the arrow in it, so he'd run, smacking right into Stu and jabbing him in the head with the protruding arrow. They'd both drop to the ground, dead...or close enough. Jackie would be so traumatized by the sight that he'd yank out all of his green hair and flee deep into the forest, never to be seen again.

Henry would look over at Max and give a sheepish grin as if to say, *Yes, I realize that I inadvertently caused a horrific bloodbath, but killing three people with a single arrow is a pretty sweet accomplishment, right?* And then a tiger, not even native to this region, would leap out of a tree and kill Erik. Then Max would explain that his insurance policy only covered him up to two camper deaths, unless he could prove that it was the work of a masked slasher, since he'd purchased extra mad slasher coverage just in case. Max would strap on a hockey mask and pull the starter cord on his motorized machete and Henry would scream and scream and scream—

But that was the worst-case scenario. Why dwell on the negative? What if he shot the arrow using flawless form and got a bull's-eye? He'd shrug, indicating to everybody that it was no big deal, and then shoot again. This arrow would split the first arrow right down the middle. Then he'd shoot two more arrows that split the two pieces of the first arrow down the middle and then four more arrows that split each of those four pieces down the middles.

This would enrage Max, because deep inside he knew that he could barely split a single arrow into two pieces, much less eight. "I'll teach you to make me look foolish!" he'd bellow, and then he'd trip, looking foolish. Everybody would point and laugh as he ran away to nurse his wounded pride.

Max held the fiberglass bow out to Henry. He took it. Seemed pretty straightforward. Not too heavy. Unlikely to snap in half and send a piece of fiberglass deep into his nostril. He could handle this.

Max handed him an arrow. "Show us what you've got."

Henry stepped over to the line and faced the target. In his peripheral vision, he could see Randy and the others backing away, but he didn't take offense. They were going to learn that he was a force to be reckoned with. He would become one with his bow and arrow. He would be the Archery Master.

He held the bow in his left hand and notched the arrow with his right. Henry pulled back the string. More tension than he'd expected, but that was okay. He could handle it, no problems here. He stared at the target, willing it to become larger, which probably wouldn't work, but again, that was okay.

He pulled the string all the way back.

He imagined Max's face on the target, which was way more legal than aiming at the real Max's face.

He was the Archery Master.

Maybe he should close his eyes and let the arrow guide itself. The spirits within the wood would find their way to the target.

No, that would be stupid. He'd shoot somebody.

"Any day now," said Max.

There had to be thousands of clever responses to that, but Henry couldn't think of any of them. He put Max out of his mind and focused on the target—that beautiful yellow bull's-eye...or that lovely ring of red around it. Even the white part would be okay. As long as he hit somewhere on the bale of hay, he could consider himself redeemed.

He released the string.

It actually hurt his fingers as the arrow launched. Not in an "Aah! Aah! The agony is unbearable!" way, but he hadn't expected it to hurt.

The arrow sailed through the air. It had not gone straight up or straight down, which was nice.

Unlike bowling, where you got to stand there watching for a few seconds, frantically trying to control the ball through sheer mind power before it went into the gutter, this was over in a split second.

Bull's-eye.

It wasn't a perfect enough bull's-eye to make him think he was the chosen one or anything. It was right on the edge of the yellow, but still, it was a bull's-eye!

He'd shot a bull's-eye! An actual bull's-eye!

He didn't even care that it wasn't the same target he'd been aiming at!

The other kids applauded. Randy gave him a respectful "Woo!"

Henry lowered the bow and looked over at Max.

"Your technique was appallingly pitiful," said Max. "But in a survival situation, all that matters are results. If a yeti is gnawing on your leg and your inept kick knocks it down the mountain, you've still knocked a yeti down the mountain. Nice work, Henry."

Henry beamed. He'd gained the approval of a madman.

"Would you like to shoot again?" asked Max.

"No, thank you, sir."

"Stu, you're up."

Unlike Henry, Stu was given actual tips on how to correctly shoot an arrow, though he missed the target on ten out of ten attempts. One of the arrows went straight into the ground in front of him, missing his shoe by a couple of feet, which wasn't all that close of a call, but it *could* have been close, and so it was a bit unnerving.

"Very disappointing," said Max, gesturing for Stu to get back in line. "Erik?"

Erik did better than zero out of ten. Eight of his shots hit the target, though none hit the center two rings.

Jackie missed nine times, but his tenth shot struck the upper-left corner of the bale of hay. He seemed satisfied with that.

As Randy walked up, he did a strut that Henry had never seen before. It wasn't a strut that contained actual *rhythm* or anything, but it did display confidence. He took the bow from Max, gave a thumbs-up to Henry, and then took his place.

Swish! "Practice shot."

Swish! "Another practice shot."

Swish! "Just getting the feel of the bow. This one is balanced different than the one that shot the suction-cup arrows."

Swish! "Practice shot."

Swish! "Hmmmm."

Swish! "Archery sucks."

Thwack! "That bird shouldn't have been there."

Swish! "Practice shot."

Swish! "Oh, God, why didn't I go help that bird? That's not the real me! I'd never act like that when a bird got hurt! I never wanted to hurt anybody! I have to see if he's okay!"

Randy rushed into the clearing, past the target, and began searching for the fallen bird.

"Did you find it?" Henry asked.

"Not yet. There's a dead bird on the ground, but I don't think it's the same one."

Henry glanced over at Max, predicting that he would look annoyed. Henry's prediction was correct.

"Found him." Randy walked back over to the boys, cradling a robin in his hands. It had some blood on its wing, but it was still breathing. "I think he's going to make it."

"Are you planning to nurse that bird back to health?" asked Max.

"Yes, sir."

"For food?"

"No, sir."

Max sighed. "If you give that bird a name, it's a McNugget."

WILDERNESS SURVIVAL TIP!

Drinking your own sweat will not save your life. Somebody might have told you that, but they were just trying to find out if you'd really do it.

CHAPTER SIX

Erik raised his hand. "Sir? Are we going to get to shoot guns?"

"Do you want to shoot guns?"

"Yes, sir."

The look of pride that came over Max's face was so intense that it was as if Erik had won a gold medal in the Olympics, rescued eighty-six children from a burning orphanage, and bit the tail right off a lion.

"We will shoot guns. Oh, yes, we will shoot guns. We will shoot guns that put little holes in things, guns that put big holes in things, and guns that make things not there anymore."

"Sweet," said Erik.

"However, most of you are not ready for the responsibility of handling that much destructive power, so the fantastic guns will have to wait until later, when I am confident that you won't shoot yourselves in the lymph nodes."

They all agreed that this decision was fair.

"You will need to master your shooting skills in order to compete in the Games, so as a teaser, you will all be shooting BB guns."

Everybody except Erik sucked at shooting BB guns.

* * *

"Sometimes you may not be fortunate enough to have a man-made weapon," said Max. "You may need to hurl a projectile, such as a rock, at your opponent. Perhaps even during the Games."

Everybody except Erik sucked at hurling projectiles.

* * *

"In a survival situation, you may need to catch fish without the benefit of a hook, line, or reel. This might even come in handy during the Games."

Everybody sucked at catching fish without a hook, line, or reel.

* * *

"Being able to climb a tree faster than a leopard can save your life. Though there are no immediate plans to include leopards in the Games, it's a skill that may serve you well."

Most of them were actually halfway decent at climbing a tree, though not faster than a leopard would have done it. Randy fell out of the tree. Fortunately, he was uninjured because he'd only made it to the first branch.

"If a real leopard were chasing you, you'd be dead," Max informed him.

"Got it," said Randy, still lying on the ground. "But getting eaten by a leopard is a pretty badass way to go, isn't it?"

"No."

* * *

Dinner sucked.

* * *

"What was it like?" Henry asked Jackie.

Jackie's face was completely pale and he just stared at his shoes. "I don't want to talk about it."

"Are you crying?"

"No, I'm not."

"It's okay if you are."

"I'm not crying, all right? I just don't want to talk about it."

"It's only an outhouse. How scary can it be?"

"*I said I don't want to talk about it!*"

* * *

The boys sat around the stack of logs that would have been a campfire if they'd been able to get one started, eating raw marshmallows. The bird, which was alert but couldn't fly, rested on Randy's leg.

"There were some victories today," said Max. "Not many of them. Mostly disappointments. Mostly shameful, crushing disappointments. But it's only been one day and you've put forth a real effort. And though I would not be proud to call any of you except Erik my son and even though we all know that Erik is going to win the Games, I think we're moving in the right direction. So get some sleep and we'll resume our training in the morning."

Everybody got up and started to walk toward the barracks, which were about half a mile away. Henry didn't think he'd ever been more exhausted in his life and couldn't wait for his head to hit that pillow. It was a very thin pillow that felt like it might be stuffed with corkscrews, but still, he couldn't wait for his head to hit it.

"Not you, Henry," said Max.

Henry stopped walking.

"You will be sleeping in less comfortable accommodations. Or had you forgotten?"

"I think I've learned from my mistakes," said Henry. "You've had us do all of this cool stuff, like archery, BB guns, fishing, climbing trees, not starting campfires…and it's changed me. I was different then. I was wrong. And I hope you can find it in your heart not to punish me for the things that a different Henry said. Sir."

Henry had *not* forgotten about the less comfortable accommodations and had mentally rehearsed this speech during the half hour that they were failing to create sparks by rubbing two sticks together. "Sir" was an ad-lib.

"No," said Max.

"No?"

"No."

"No, as in…?"

"No, as in, I cannot find it in my heart."

"C'mon, it's been a long day and I just want to get some sleep. Punish me tomorrow."

"This is not punishment. This is training. You will be sleeping outdoors."

"He mouthed off to you to defend me," said Randy, "so I'll sleep outside too."

"No," said Max.

"No?"

"No."

"Why not?"

"Because this is something your friend must do alone."

Randy's shoulders slumped. "I'm not sure he'll make it, sir."

"I'll be fine," Henry assured his friend. "Don't worry about me. You enjoy your cot with all of its…softness."

The other kids resumed their walk to the barracks. Randy gave one last forlorn look over his shoulder, as if they might never see each other again, except in death, and then disappeared into the darkness.

"Where am I going to sleep?" asked Henry.

Max pointed to the ground. "Right here. It's nature's Sleep Number mattress."

That wasn't as bad as Henry had expected. He'd thought that he might be sleeping in a spiked pit with some cobras. "Okay. Can I have a blanket at least?"

"You get a sleeping bag. Despite what you might believe, Henry, I don't want you to die. I'm not here to torture you. In the morning, when you wake up and realize that you've successfully slept by yourself out in the wilderness, I think you'll discover that you have a lot of unlocked potential."

"Thank you, sir."

Max patted him on the shoulder. "You'll be fine. I will, however, leave you with a bow and arrow...just in case."

*　*　*

Henry lay in his sleeping bag in the darkness. The bow and arrows did not make him feel safer. In fact, he was sort of worried that he might roll over onto them while he slept. He'd eased this fear by putting them about ten feet away, but then he worried that they wouldn't be close enough if he woke up in the middle of the night in danger. Then he remembered his bull's-eye had been total luck and having the bow and arrows nearby probably wouldn't do him much good anyway—unless he was just naturally lucky with bows and arrows, in which case they *would* do him some good. So he had to weigh the odds of rolling onto sharp, pointy arrows versus the odds of waking up with a ferocious beast about to make him a meal. Henry had to admit that the more realistic danger would be waking up with an appendix full of arrows, so he kept them out of rolling range.

He stared up at the stars. They were beautiful. He didn't really see them very often. He tried to identify the different constellations, like Sagittarius, the archer. He couldn't see anything that looked much like an archer with a horse body, but maybe you needed to chug a few cans of Red Bull first.

He tried to find the one that looked like a crab. Were there crabs out in the woods? Probably not. Even if there were crab-spawning ponds around here, the crabs wouldn't make it this far away from the water.

There was also Aries, the ram. Even at his maximum level of "I'm gonna get eaten!" paranoia, Henry wasn't worried about being attacked in these woods by a wild ram.

Of course, it would be a terrible irony if he found himself impaled by a ram, the one animal he was almost positive wasn't lurking in these woods. Maybe he *should* fear them.

No, it wasn't going to happen. His chances of encountering a ram were about the same as his chances of encountering a ghost.

Crap. There were probably ghosts everywhere in these woods.

Ghosts watching him right now.

Ghosts of those who'd died badly, who sought vengeance for the way they'd exited this plane of existence. Ghosts who were searching for a soul to possess, perhaps that of a sixteen-year-old boy lying helplessly outside with only a sleeping bag as protection against the spectral dangers.

Henry stopped looking at the stars and rolled over on his side. He was way too old to be worrying about ghosts. In fact, though he often wondered why he wasn't lucky enough to have a girlfriend, it was possible that this provided a very specific clue as to the root cause.

Something rustled in the trees.

Henry sat up.

The rustling continued.

It's just an armadillo, he told himself. *No big deal. You see squished armadillos on the side of the road all the time and they aren't going to cause you any harm.*

He scrambled out of his sleeping bag and fumbled around in the dark until he found the bow.

There was a sudden beam of light.

A ghost!

A ghost or a flashlight! One of the two!

Psycho killers with flashlights!

He hurriedly grabbed an arrow and notched it. Then he spun around.

A dark-haired girl his age stood there. She was the most beautiful potential psycho killer Henry had ever seen.

WILDERNESS SURVIVAL TIP!

If you need to start a fire, you can burn the pages of this very book. Yes, you'll hurt the author's feelings, but that's okay. Your life is more important. (If you're reading this as an e-book, setting it on fire is not recommended.)

CHAPTER SEVEN

"Hey, whoa, whoa," she said, holding up her hands to show that she was not carrying a knife or a throwable cactus. "Chill. Put down the bow."

Henry set the bow and arrow back down on the ground. This could be some sort of test that Max had set up, but even so, Henry thought it best not to risk accidentally killing a beautiful girl. (Or for that matter even an average- or below-average-looking girl.) (Or even a dog-ugly one.) (You really shouldn't kill girls, period.)

"Sorry," he said.

"Kind of jumpy, aren't you?"

"You could have been a bear."

"Oh, well, that's flattering. I guess I forgot to shave my legs this morning."

"No, I meant—"

"That I'm gigantic?"

"No."

"That I give off a bearlike scent?"

"No."

She smiled. "I'm just messing with you. Though you do know that bears don't use flashlights very often, right?"

"Yes, I know that."

"Oh, good." She walked over and crouched down next to the unlit campfire. "My name is Monica."

"I'm Henry."

"Nice to meet you, Henry. So you're part of that survival camp thing?"

"Yes."

"Is it any good?"

"Not really."

"That's too bad. I'd love to have done that. Not to brag or anything, but I'm a vicious fighter. My older brothers are terrified of me. Nice underwear by the way."

Henry flinched. He quickly decided that leaping back into the sleeping bag with a yelp would be more awkward than just being there in his underwear, so he stayed where he was. At least he was wearing boxer shorts that were not embarrassing in their style or their condition.

She was wearing jeans and a blue T-shirt. Her hair was cut short. She had the body of a gymnast, which Henry thought was an excellent kind of body to have.

"Thank you," he said. He tried to think of a clever follow-up comment (*I sewed them myself. They're bulletproof. I bought them with my own money. They used to glow in the dark.*) but rejected all of his ideas. "Are you from the music camp?"

"Yep."

"I didn't realize it was that close."

"It's about three miles away."

"You walked three miles?"

Monica shrugged. "I like to walk at night. I find it relaxing. Don't you find it relaxing?"

"Yes," said Henry, who most certainly did not find the idea of walking at night relaxing.

"Why are you out here alone? Do you snore?"

"I gave attitude to the leader." Henry hoped this made him sound dangerous.

"Why?"

"He tried to make my friend do push-ups."

"Not in favor of push-ups?"

"I'm okay with the concept of push-ups," Henry told her, promising himself that this would be his final lie of the night. "But he was a jerk about it."

"Did you call him a jerk to his face?"

Henry almost went back on his promise from two seconds ago, but he figured that the odds were pretty good that he'd do something cowardly before she left and give away the lie, so he might as well be honest. "Nah."

"I don't blame you. It's that guy in that one video, right? The Steroid Avenger?"

"Yeah, he's a little intense. So I have to sleep out here tonight. It's not that big of a deal."

It occurred to Henry that this was the longest continuous one-on-one conversation he'd ever had with a girl this beautiful. No, wait. There was his freshman-year lab partner, Charlene. So this was the longest continuous one-on-one conversation he'd ever had with a girl this beautiful that didn't end with him accidentally spilling hydrochloric acid on her blouse.

"Do you have to sleep out here every night or just tonight?"

"Hopefully just tonight."

"Oh. Well, if you give him attitude again, I'll see you tomorrow night."

"You're leaving already?"

Monica shrugged. "I don't have to, I guess. I left my bunkmates a note not to freak out if they woke up and I was gone. Is it okay if I start the fire?"

"Can you do that?" Henry asked. "We tried with sticks all evening and we couldn't even get them to smoke."

Monica took out a lighter, flicked on the flame, and lit the tinder.

"Well, yeah, that works too. We aren't allowed to have modern stuff. What instrument do you play?"

"Clarinet."

"Do you like it?"

"It's kind of hard to rock out on a clarinet, but it's fine. It makes my parents happy. I may or may not keep it up after I graduate. Haven't decided yet. Do you play an instrument?"

"I'm awesome at *Guitar Hero*."

"That almost counts."

"And I would destroy you in a battle of the kazoos. *Destroy* you." Henry hadn't played a kazoo in years, but he didn't think it was a skill that you lost.

"I have a kazoo right here, so I call your bluff."

"Seriously?"

"No."

"Oh, I *thought* you were joking, but you never know. Some people carry kazoos around just in case. Like clowns. Clowns carry kazoos, I think." *Babbling sequence: off,* thought Henry as he shut up.

"If we ever do find ourselves together with a pair of kazoos handy, I accept your challenge." She blew into the fire, spreading the flames nicely.

Henry loved talking to her and really wished he wasn't in his underwear. There was no dignity in this. He wasn't comfortable with his body and couldn't pull off the whole "Oh, yeah, babe, you *know* you like what you see" vibe.

"Which school do you go to?" he asked.

"Baver. You?"

"Flagston." Of course. It would have been too much to hope that they went to the same school and had just missed each other in the hallways all this time.

She smiled. "So technically, you're my arch-nemesis. Sleep with one eye open, Henry."

Monica's leg buzzed.

"Who's texting me at one in the morning?" she wondered aloud, taking her cell phone out of her pocket. She glanced at the display and laughed. "Ah, my friends are such dorks." She tucked the phone back into her pocket.

"Was that a cell phone?" Henry asked.

"Yes. Have you not seen one before? They're a pretty sweet means of communication."

"No, I knew what it was, I was just—Do you have any games on it?"

"I'm not that much into video games," she said. It was a combination of words that would normally cause Henry to shudder with revulsion, but coming from Monica they didn't sound so bad. It was okay. They could work through this.

"Do you have any?"

"I think there's something where you match up coins."

"Can I match up coins on your phone?" Henry asked. "I won't use up your battery or run off with it, I promise. One game. That's it."

She shrugged and handed him the phone. He swiped through her weirdly small selection of apps until he found *Coin Join*. The graphics were from about six years ago. The sounds were nothing but annoying beeps and the gameplay seemed like it had been designed for people who took pride in their own stupidity, but oooohhhhhh, the bliss!

Oh, yeah, look at those coins. Look at those coins match. Oh, baby, those were some great digital coins.

Henry glanced over his shoulder, as if Max might be looming above him, snarling with rage. But he wasn't.

As Henry sat there, matching multicolored coins, he realized that today hadn't been such a bad day. Sure, there'd been humiliation and discomfort and gross food, yet he'd talked to a gorgeous girl without her—to the best of his knowledge—thinking he was a total loser. Right now, he was sitting next to her by the campfire, playing a video game. The only thing to make it more perfect would be if he had some Cheetos and a highly caffeinated beverage.

Okay, it would be more perfect if she jumped him. That could wait until they'd known each other more than a few minutes.

Life was awesome.

As he got a quadruple coin match on a triple space, which earned him big points, a text message popped up on the screen from somebody named Lydia. *Bobby sez he misses your hot bod! Come home or he's mine LOL!*

Well...crap.

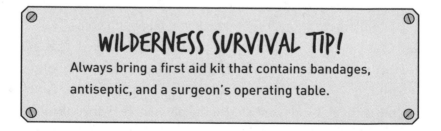

WILDERNESS SURVIVAL TIP!

Always bring a first aid kit that contains bandages, antiseptic, and a surgeon's operating table.

CHAPTER EIGHT

Somebody knocked.

Larry Dexter's stomach immediately cramped up. Knocks weren't a good thing. He was never happy to see the person on the other side of the door.

He wanted to go hide in the bathroom and pretend that he wasn't home, but the TV was on, so they knew he was here. This would go a lot worse if they had to break in. He set his bowl of soggy cereal on the coffee table, brushed off his shirt and pants, ran a hand through his hair, and took a deep breath. Maybe it was just somebody selling something. He walked over and opened the door.

It wasn't Girl Scouts.

"Mr. Grand!" he said. "Good to see you, buddy!"

There were two other men with Mr. Grand. Larry recognized them but didn't know their names. Mr. Grand's associates tended not to introduce themselves.

"Are you going to invite us in?" asked Mr. Grand.

"Oh, yes, yes, of course. Come on in."

The three men entered Larry's apartment. The last one in closed the door behind him.

"It reeks in here," said Mr. Grand with a mild grimace. "Don't you have any respect for yourself? What kind of a man would live in filth like this?"

Larry shrugged. "Maid's day off," he said.

Mr. Grand did not smile. Mr. Grand was not a man who appreciated humor.

Larry cleared his throat and gestured to the couch. "Please... have a seat."

"Thank you, but we won't be sitting on your plague-infested sofa."

"Can I get you a drink?"

"Nor will we be drinking anything that was in this disease hole. We may even make you pay for the clothes we'll have to burn after we leave here. Are you going to turn down the TV or do I have to put a bullet in it?"

Larry gave him a nervous chuckle. "I'll go you one better." After a moment of searching, he found the remote and turned the TV off completely. "That okay?"

"It's fine."

"Good, good. So to what do I owe the pleasure of your visit?"

Mr. Grand was a big guy and he looked even bigger when he was angry. "Are you telling me that you're going to make me suffer through this stench *and* insult my intelligence?"

"No, not at all. The money, right?"

"Yes, Lester. The money."

Larry despised being called Lester but wasn't about to correct him. He was sweating like crazy and really wished he'd put on deodorant this week. "Yeah, about that—"

"If you say you don't have the money, you are going to die tonight. It's as simple as that."

"No, that's not what I was saying at all. Nothing like that."

"Then go get it."

"It's not *here*. I mean, my place is a dump—I'm man enough to admit that. I wouldn't hide a bunch of cash here."

"Then take us to it," said Mr. Grand. "We have nowhere else to be tonight."

"Right. Thing is…my cash is tied up in investments. You know me. I'm a businessman. You've gotta make your money work for you. You understand, right?"

Mr. Grand sighed. "You're going to make us break your legs, aren't you?"

"No! You can't believe how much money I've got coming in. Soon. Real soon. I've got this thing, this survival camp for teenagers. They're crazy for it. Hundreds of kids are there. They're turning them away by the dozens. We could run these sessions all year long and not keep up with the demand. There's this guy Max who runs it, and once he gives me my cut, I can pay you back, plus interest, plus a tip. I'd take you right over there, but he's up in Wisconsin. He's the one you should be going after, not me."

"You say his name is Max?"

Larry vigorously nodded.

"Is he a friend of yours?"

"Yeah, yeah, sure he is. Good guy, good guy."

"So you're sending people like us after somebody you consider a friend?"

"Yeah, I mean, you want your money, right?"

"I ask again, Lester. What kind of a man are you?"

Larry's mouth went dry, and his need for deodorant tripled. "Just trying to make sure you get paid is all."

"I see," said Mr. Grand. "Do you want to know the only reason that I'm not going to kill you right now?"

"Okay."

"Because if I killed you, we'd have to dispose of your disgusting body, and even though I wouldn't be doing it myself, I respect my men too much to subject them to that."

Larry breathed a deep sigh of relief.

"We will be back soon," said Mr. Grand. "I expect to you have the money."

"Will do. Absolutely. You've got it."

"If not, we will kill you. It will take a long time. Do you understand?"

"Yes."

"Good. And clean this place up."

Mr. Grand and his men left. Larry plopped down on the couch, had another bite of soggy cereal, and then spent the rest of the evening softly weeping.

CHAPTER EIGHT AND A HALF

"Hey, Henry! How's it going?"

"What are you doing in here? I thought security dragged you away!"

"Hey, Rad Rad Roger isn't gonna let a couple of muscle-bound goons keep him from his job! Using the bathroom during the movie, huh? I have to do that when I get nervous too."

"Get that camera out of here! I'm peeing!"

"We'll blur it."

"You said this was live!"

"I'd like to ask you about Max. In the movie, he's played by Katy Perry, which seems like an odd casting choice. Care to comment?"

"Yeah, there was some retooling of his character. Hollywood, you know."

"Was he really as crazy as he sounded in the book, or was there some creative license there as well?"

"Yeah, he was one crazy guy, and it was pretty accurate. Maybe not everything he said was word for word how it appeared in the book, but overall, yeah, that was Max."

"I've got the book right here. Tell me, Henry. How did you know what happened when Mr. Grand and his goons came to visit Larry Dexter at his apartment? You weren't there, were you? I mean, I don't remember reading a scene where you left camp, drove all the way to Larry's house in a different state, hid in Larry's closet, waited for everybody to leave, and then drove all the way back to camp."

"Well, I didn't write the book."

"You didn't?"

"No."

"I thought you did."

"No, my name's not on the cover."

"Oh. You're right. My bad. Anyway, when are the Games going to start? When you watch *The Hunger Games*, the actual Games start, like, three minutes into the movie."

"That's not correct at all."

"Maybe I'm thinking of something else."

"You probably are."

"You're right, you're right. When I was watching *The Hunger Games*, I kept checking my watch and going, 'Damn, how long is it gonna take them to get to the stupid Hunger Games part?' That movie bored me silly. What'd you think?"

"I loved the movie and the book."

"There was a book?"

"Yes."

"How'd I miss that?"

"I don't know."

"So let's get back to your book. Were *you* portrayed in an accurate manner in the book?"

"Yeah, I think so. The author worked with me pretty closely."

"I peeked into the movie for a few seconds and you broke a kid's neck. Punched him right in the face and snapped his neck. I missed the setup, but the audience laughed, so I guess it was funny. Was that part accurate?"

"No, I'd be in jail if that really happened."

"So the book portrayed you in a more accurate manner than the movie?"

"Yeah."

"Like I said, I haven't read the whole thing yet, but in the book you're kind of a wuss."

"I disagree with that."

"Total wuss."

"You're trying to get me mad on camera. Go away or I'll report you."

"Not proving your lack of wussdom, Henry."

"I've gotta get back to the movie."

CHAPTER NINE

Henry didn't say anything about the text message. He matched five purple coins in a diagonal row but felt no real elation about this mighty accomplishment.

He closed out of the game and handed the phone back to Monica. "Thanks," he said. "I really needed that."

She tucked the phone back into her pocket. "No problem. Now I really do have to get back. I hope you survive the night so I can see you tomorrow."

"Me too."

She stood up, gave him a smile that made ninety-three percent of the feeling vanish from his legs, and then headed back on the path from which she came. Henry watched her until she disappeared completely into the darkness. He didn't like seeing her leave, but it was a spectacular view.

Monica had a boyfriend. That made sense. Girls who looked like her didn't typically have much difficulty finding a suitable mating partner.

He'd thought she was being a bit flirty, but when he replayed the conversation in his mind, he decided that she was just being friendly.

He replayed the conversation again. Yep. Friendly, not flirty.

He replayed the conversation once more because even if she hadn't been flirting, it was a very pleasant memory.

Maybe there was trouble in paradise. After all, why hadn't Bobby texted her himself? Did he not miss her enough? Was he lazy? There was absolutely no reason in the world for that lazy jerk not to be texting her himself. Except—

1. He might not own a cell phone.
2. He might own a cell phone but not have it with him at the moment.
3. He might own a cell phone, but the battery died.
4. He might own a cell phone, but because he was out too late with Monica, doing amazing things, he missed curfew and his parents took the cell phone away from him for a week.
5. He might have been texting her all day constantly, texting things that were pure poetry, using emoticons like a true artist. At some point, his thumbs had to give out.
6. It was one in the morning. Some people slept at that time.

Henry didn't like any of those. Much better reasons were—

1. Every time Bobby texted, he said something stupid, like "LUV UR BOOBIES HUH HUH HUH." Monica was getting tired of it and told him that if he didn't have something intelligent to text, not to text her at all, so he chose not to text her at all.
2. He was such a hopeless klutz that every time he got a new cell phone, he'd drop it in a puddle of water. Right now his phone was in a bowl of dry rice, even though the dry rice trick to save a wet phone didn't actually work. Monica was getting tired of his klutziness. What she really wanted was a master archer.
3. Bobby did not exist. Upon seeing Henry, Monica had contacted one of her friends and said, "There's a really cute guy

here, and I want to make him jealous. Send me a text that makes it look like I have a boyfriend."

4. Bobby was in prison. His nickname was "Mad Dog Bobby" and he was currently serving a fifty-year sentence. He'd killed a man just to finger-paint a picture of a duck with his blood. Monica wanted to be true to him, her first and only boyfriend, but deep inside, she knew that she was simply waiting for her dream man to show up. Yes, when Henry turned sixty-six, he knew that he'd have to deal with Mad Dog Bobby's desire for revenge, but he'd worry about that later.

5. Bobby was a total snob who felt that texting was only for the illiterate. He communicated with Monica only through the things he wrote upon a cloth scroll with a quill dipped in ink. Monica was getting tired of it.

6. Bobby was a lazy jerk.

Henry was cool with any of those scenarios. Perhaps number four was a bit unlikely, but the others—

Okay, he knew that she was a beautiful girl with a (probably) nice boyfriend who (probably) adored her and who she (probably but hopefully not) adored in return. Guys like Henry did not have girlfriends of her caliber unless they were in a band and guys like Henry were not usually in a band. But somehow, he had to be able to win her over.

She liked long hikes in the dark scary outdoors, so she was a woodsy type. If Henry *dominated* survival camp, if he showed that he knew his way around a campfire and whatever else the great wilderness threw at him, if he won the Games, it might impress her.

That was it. For the next week and six days, he'd devote himself to being the ultimate survivalist. When they got to the big competition at the end, Randy, Erik, Jackie, and Stu would all fear him.

This he vowed.

* * *

When he woke up, an armadillo was about three inches from his face, staring at him. Henry screamed.

* * *

Breakfast sucked.

* * *

"In a survival situation, a shelter is of maximum importance," said Max. "You cannot defend yourself against hordes of vampires—and I, of course, am speaking completely hypothetically—if you have already frozen to death."

Jackie raised his hand. "Sir?"

"Yes?"

"Are we likely to freeze to death in June?"

"I'm about to ask you something, Jackie, and I want you to be completely honest with me: Do you believe that was an intelligent question?"

"I didn't think it was that bad."

"It was. It was very bad. You know that old saying 'The only stupid question is one not asked'? It's the saying itself that is stupid. You are always welcome to ask questions here, but I encourage you to spend one or two seconds appraising the question first. Otherwise, you might ask something that implies that you believe that the only possible time in the entire world that you could ever find yourself needing a shelter is in June. When it's only seven thirty in the morning and I've already heard a question that I know will be one of the top three dumbest questions of the day, it depresses me."

Jackie hung his head. "I'm sorry, sir."

Jackie really wished he hadn't asked his question. It had seemed like a smart question when he asked it. Not smart like Einstein asking a question about physics but smart enough to prove to Max that he was paying attention. As soon as Max started griping, he'd realized that, yeah, it wasn't the best question he'd ever asked, but by then, it was too late to un-ask it. And now everybody thought he was that green-haired kid who asked dumb questions.

It would've been different if they thought of him as that *weird* green-haired kid. If he was going to be an outcast, he wanted everybody to think he was an outcast because of his fashion choice. Unfortunately, nobody seemed to think that his green hair was all that strange.

Sure, his grandmother hated it. "Why would you disfigure yourself like that?" she'd ask. But it didn't count if it only upset your grandma. His parents had the attitude of "Well, at least he isn't holding up convenience stores or setting fire to anything" and even bought him the green stuff.

He hated being an outcast. Yeah, the other boys were all pretty nice to him. But his plan to win them over via his possessions had been ruined, and last night, he hadn't felt like he was contributing his share to the conversation about whether or not everybody thought Henry would be dead by morning. Jackie knew he was an outcast, even though they were letting him be a full member of their social group.

He would still ask questions. But Max's rule about thinking about them for one or two seconds beforehand seemed reasonable.

"Anybody else have any questions?" asked Max.

There was silence for a moment. Then Erik raised his hand.

"Yes, Erik?"

"You mentioned vampires. Would vampires really be an issue in a cold-weather environment? I know there was that one movie based on that one graphic novel, but if we were in a place where we were worried about freezing to death, I don't think vampires would be much of a threat."

"Vampires don't exist, Erik. You realize that, right?"

"Yes, sir. Sorry, sir."

There were no other dumb questions, at least none that were spoken out loud.

Erik, of course, did not believe in vampires. He did, however, believe that there were people who believed in vampires and it concerned him that Max might be one of them.

Erik was, deep in his heart, a nerd. A closeted nerd. His handsome face, athletic build, and above-average skills at physical activities made him feel that he should hide his true nature, but he knew he was a nerd. He longed to join a *Dungeons & Dragons* club. Dreamt of going to a science-fiction convention in costume. Dreamt of somebody saying "Hey, nice *Doctor Who* costume!" so that he could give them a derisive snort and say "*Doctor Who* is the name of the show, not the character. He's just 'The Doctor.' Any true fan would know that."

He loved monsters. Vampires, zombies, mummies, wolfmen, Bigfeet, swamp creatures, ghosts, witches, carnivorous pugs, dragons, orcs, possessed children, chupacabras, koala bears with fangs—he loved them all. Loved them so much that it really bothered him when other people took these monsters too seriously and ruined it for everybody else.

Erik wanted to learn useful survival skills, but he didn't want to learn them from a nutcase who thought vampires were going to bite them while they built a shelter. He thought Max might actually have a zombie apocalypse preparedness plan worked out for real and those were the kinds of people who made Erik feel that he had to try out for the football team, even though he secretly wanted to play chess.

Max rolled his eyes. "Can we discuss the actual construction of shelters now?"

Everybody nodded.

"Stu," said Max. "If your plane crashed and you found yourself stranded out here, what resources could you expect to obtain from the woods?"

Stu considered that. "Well, I guess I'd start by seeing what I could get from the plane wreckage."

"The plane wreckage doesn't count. Natural resources only."

"You mean I'd just leave all of the plane stuff behind?"

"Yes."

"Why would I do that?"

"Because our topic for today is how to build a shelter out of the resources you find in the wilderness."

"Yeah, but if there's a whole plane's worth of stuff, I'd use that before I started knocking down trees."

"The plane exploded on impact, scattering burning chunks of metal for miles. You're lucky to have survived."

"I'd still be more inclined to search for useful pieces of wreckage."

"The other passengers were so annoyed by you that they voted in favor of opening the door in midflight and throwing you out. The two or three people who were sucked out with you and plummeted to their deaths felt it was worth the sacrifice. You survived, but the plane and its useful components are long gone."

"Am I injured?"

"Do you want to be?"

"No."

"That's smart."

"Okay, so if I was trying to use natural resources to build a shelter, I guess I'd start with...wood?"

"Yes. Wood is a fine place to start."

"I'd get a bunch of wood. Branches, those are a good source of wood. Maybe a log that somebody else left there. Leaves too. They're probably already on the branches, so you'd just have to remember not to start taking them off. If it started raining, you'd want to have leaves because water doesn't go through leaves. I don't think you'd need rocks. Would you need rocks?"

"Probably not."

"Yeah, that's what I was thinking. If you wanted to make a path to your shelter, maybe you'd use rocks, but that would be something for the second or third day. You wouldn't start with that."

"No. You wouldn't."

"Bones. If you found some bones, they could help. You could use them to prop up the structure. Not bird bones, but if it was something big that had bones, you could use them sort of the way you'd use the wood, except that it would be stronger. You couldn't cut it as easily, so you'd keep them in their original shape. Like if you found ribs, you'd keep them shaped like ribs. You wouldn't break them or anything. Or maybe you would. I guess if you broke them into tiny pieces, you could use them to make a path to your shelter, but like I already said, that wouldn't be a priority. And you'd need to make sure that everybody in your party had good shoes because you wouldn't want to walk on broken bones without good shoes."

"Of course not."

"A tarp. Not a naturally occurring plastic tarp but something in nature that you could use as a tarp. I guess that's what the leaves would've been for. I don't know what else you would use. Sunlight? I don't know."

"Are you finished?" Max asked.

"Yes, sir. I do want to clarify that I wouldn't start looking for bones first thing. I would use the branches and leaves first. It would be more that if I *found* some bones while I was looking for the other stuff, I would try to put them to practical use, not that I would instantly start digging for bones as soon as the plane crashed."

"Good to know."

"That's basically my answer."

"I got it."

"If it's not the answer you wanted, I can change it."

"No, I think we're okay, Stu." Max stood there for a few moments, looking sad, but then he composed himself. "For this shelter-building exercise, you will be divided into two teams."

What Max said next was like a roaring chainsaw of pure fear in everybody's heart, except maybe Erik's.

WILDERNESS SURVIVAL TIP!

If you're sinking in quicksand, it is very important not to shout, "Help! I'm sinking in quicksand!" Because if your friends think there's quicksand around, no way are they going to be dumb enough to try to pull you out and risk getting stuck themselves. Instead, you should shout, "Help! This natural hot springs is so comfortable that I feel guilty enjoying it all by myself!"

CHAPTER TEN

Schoolyard pick.

There was nothing more cruel. Nothing more evil.

By his calculations, Henry was picked last for sports approximately forty-five percent of the time. The only reason the percentage wasn't higher was that Randy sometimes got picked after him.

When a new kid named Frank had moved to his school from Seattle, Henry had been secretly thrilled because Frank had an artificial leg. Unfortunately for Henry, Frank turned out to not only be the fastest runner in the class but a bully who liked to kick weaker kids with his artificial leg.

With only five people to choose from, Henry didn't think it would be *too* humiliating to be picked last for the shelter-building teams, but this wasn't how he wanted to start his new era of dominating the camp.

"Stu," said Max, "pick a number between one and ten."

"One."

"One?"

"Yes, sir."

"You realize that if somebody else picks two, they get all of the numbers between two and ten, right?"

Stu nodded.

"Henry, pick a number between one and ten."

"Two."

Stu cursed.

"Randy, pick a number between one and ten."

"Two."

"Was he allowed to pick the same number?" asked Erik.

"No, he disqualified himself. Erik, pick a number between one and ten."

"Five."

"Excellent choice. But the number was one. Stu and Henry, you're the team captains. Henry, make your first and only selection."

"Randy."

Max glared at him. "With all due respect, I think we can all agree that Randy is not your best possible option. Please explain your reasoning."

"He's my best friend," said Henry.

"And that automatically makes him the best shelter-builder?"

"No," said Henry, thankful that he had blurted out Randy's name before he stopped to seriously consider who might be best at the task, which would have plunged him into a moral quandary about the loyalty of friendship versus the end goal to be achieved. He wanted to win, but he wasn't going to dump Randy to help him achieve that goal. Only a total jerk would do that. He was a nerd, not a jerk.

Max nodded. "In a survival situation, it is often more important to have people who are trustworthy than people who are competent. You don't want to share a shelter with somebody who will try to feed you to whatever might be trying to eat you. Well done."

"Thank you, sir."

"Stu? Your pick."

"Aw, man." Stu looked back and forth between Erik and Jackie. "I feel like Erik is probably stronger—"

"*Probably* stronger?" asked Erik.

"But Jackie would take up less room in the shelter, so we wouldn't have to make the shelter quite as big. Then again, Jackie's hair would be more likely to stain the pillows, unless we use leaves for pillows, in which case he would just be staining the leaves the same color that they already are."

"*Probably* stronger?" Erik repeated.

"Hey, it's not like I've seen you two arm wrestle," said Stu.

"Make your pick," said Max.

"Okay, the person I choose for my team is…umm…*Jackie.*" Jackie beamed.

"…Stay in line," Stu continued, "because I pick Erik."

"Aw, dude," said Jackie. "That wasn't a cool way to do it."

"Yeah, you're right. I change my pick to Jackie."

"You don't get to change your pick," said Max.

"Okay, good."

"Jackie, since you were picked last, you will be given the most important task. You are now the sabotage crew. At certain brief intervals, you will be allowed to destroy the hard work that your fellow campers have done."

"*Sweet!*"

"Here's how this is going to work," said Max. "You will have one hour to build a shelter. The team that does the best job of constructing a shelter in which you could spend the night and not die is the winner."

"What do we win?" asked Henry.

"You win the gift of potentially not being dead. Also, the losing team has to make lunch. The competition begins…now!"

Erik whispered something to Stu and they immediately took

off running. What did Erik know that Henry didn't? Was there a Home Depot nearby?

Randy held the injured bird, wrapped in a blue cloth, and gently stroked the top of its head with his thumb. "We could try for an underground one, if you can dig really fast," he said.

"I can't dig really fast."

"A lean-to then?"

"Sure."

"Do you know how to make one?"

"I can't even visualize a lean-to," said Henry. "I'm picturing something, but I think it's a teepee."

"We may be screwed on the lean-to idea then."

"Why didn't you look it up before we got here?"

"I thought they were going to *teach* us survival skills! I purposely *didn't* look up how to build a shelter because I thought the instructor would appreciate me being a clean slate! Otherwise, I would've been all like, 'No, no, that's not how Wikipedia says to do it.' Why didn't *you* look it up before we got here?"

"We can't turn against each other," said Henry. "That's what Erik and Stu and maybe Jackie want us to do. We've got to work together. If we work together, what do you think the odds are of us finding a cave?"

"Poor."

"I agree. Okay, so however we build the shelter, we're going to need branches. Let's get lots of branches."

Randy nodded. They searched for the nearest branch-producing object, which was not a time-consuming task since they were in the woods.

Henry found a tree that had at least twenty or thirty accessible branches that looked perfect for building the shelter he couldn't visualize. They didn't have a chainsaw, hacksaw, machete, pocketknife, butcher knife, steak knife, tin can lid, sharpened teeth, or anything else that would help them to saw off the branches, but suddenly, Henry got an idea.

He walked over to where Max and Jackie stood, watching them. "Sir?"

"Yes?"

"Can you spare a grenade, sir?"

"Why?"

"In a survival situation, having a grenade to blow off a bunch of branches can save time."

"I like the way you think," said Max. "But a criminal level of irresponsibility can only be taken so far and I have to say no."

"Well, sir," said Henry, not giving up, "nothing would be a greater honor than to watch you explode the branches for us."

"Are you patronizing me, you little puke?"

"No, sir. I'm here to learn."

"Pig, horse, and bull crap. Jackie, sabotage their shelter."

"They haven't started it yet, sir."

"Then pee on the ground where they're going to build it."

"I don't have to go, sir."

"Forget it then." Max looked at Henry and then cracked his knuckles in such a way to clearly send the message: *Pretend that my knuckles are your neck. Or your spine. Either one works.* "Do not try to outwit me. I'm smarter than I look. And I'm smart enough to know that you're thinking, 'That's not very hard to do.' Go on. Think it if you weren't already."

Henry was already thinking it. It was extremely difficult to keep his face from giving that away.

"I could probably pee now," said Jackie.

"Nah, save it. Henry, get back to your shelter."

"He won't let us blow up the tree," Henry said, walking back over to Randy.

"Oh well." Randy had only gotten three branches off. They were going to have to work faster than that if they expected to win, although Henry didn't say this, because it could be interpreted as a similar comment to the "Why didn't you look it up before we got here?" one, which had been poorly received.

Randy had laid the cloth out on the ground. The bird chirped. Henry wasn't sure if the bird was offering moral support or insulting him.

Henry grabbed one of the lower branches. "Ow," he said.

"What?"

"Nothing."

"You shouldn't grab the poky part."

"I didn't know there was a poky part." Henry grabbed the branch and tugged a few times. It wouldn't come free.

"Dude, are you trying to pull off the branch or are you trying to milk it?"

"What's wrong with the way I'm doing it?"

"You have to pull down or twist it or use your foot. You really don't know how to pull off a branch? Even by my standards that's lame."

Henry had to admit that for somebody who was sixteen years old instead of three, it was a pretty feeble effort. But why should he know how to debranch a tree? He lived in a world where wood was conveniently cut for you. He had his own set of skills. After all, how many lumberjacks could…?

After a moment of thought, he realized that he didn't really have any skills that were out of reach for a lumberjack.

He yanked the branch again, pulling downward. This was an improvement in that the branch felt more likely to come off than his arms did, but it still wasn't all that productive. He worked at it for a few more moments. The branch didn't come loose. He couldn't help but feel that he wasn't dominating the camp to quite the extent that he'd intended.

Randy pressed his foot against a branch and kicked down a few times until the branch came off the tree.

Henry pressed his foot against a branch and kicked down a few times until the branch remained exactly where it was.

Randy must've been working on a thinner branch or he had heavier shoes. Henry continued to kick. He almost jumped up onto it, but knew that would not end well.

"Gosh darn it all to heck," he said, approximately.

He was getting mad, but that was good because he needed adrenaline. In fact, he tried to think angry thoughts, like "Evil exists in the world" or "Nobody makes good chimpanzee movies anymore."

Clearly, he had been unfortunate enough to pick the one tree in the forest made out of solid steel. He hoped that Max wasn't watching him, but Henry knew deep in his heart that he was. Max was standing there, shaking his head sadly, wondering where humanity had gone wrong, wondering how evolution and/or creationism had come up with something like Henry.

The madder Henry got, the harder he tried, and the exact amount the branch continued not to come off the tree. Henry's was not a life devoid of embarrassment and this probably wasn't even *Henry Lambert: His Top Ten Biggest Moments of Shame* material, but still, he needed this to stop.

"As team captain, I've decided to delegate," he told Randy. "Your job is to keep breaking off the branches because I'm less awesome at it than you are. My job is to find us a good tree to use for the shelter."

Randy pointed at a large tree. "That one's perfect."

"There might be better ones."

"You don't know a good lean-to tree from a bad lean-to tree."

"Actually…do you even use a tree for a lean-to shelter? I think I'm finally picturing one. The branches aren't leaning against a tree."

Randy's face fell. "You're right. And we're going to need bigger branches."

Henry successfully kept his wail of eternal torment on the inside. "Okay," he said, though the word sounded more like "aacchk."

"Do you want to go see what Erik and Stu are doing?"

Was ripping off other people's ideas okay in a survival situation? Henry started to nod but changed his head movement to side-to-side shaking instead. "If we're going to win, I want to win fairly. And if we're going to lose, at least we lost with dignity."

"What dignity?" Randy asked. "There's no dignity here."

"I mean the dignity of not having cheated. Maybe that's too strong of a word. Anyway, I'm going to look for a—"

Henry did not have anything specific in mind that he was going to look for and had hoped that an idea would occur to him between the time that he said, "I'm going to look for a—". and the time it was necessary to complete the sentence. Instead, he was distracted from his sentence-finishing when he stepped on a branch.

It was a very sharp branch but not sharp enough to go through his shoe and cause any kind of foot-jabbing injury. It was merely sharp enough to make him stumble a bit and step on a second branch.

The big problem with this second branch was that it was shaped sort of like a garden rake. Now, if you were to attempt to use it to rake up leaves or piles of newly mown grass, it would be a very inefficient tool. You'd quickly get frustrated, possibly use some foul language if that's your thing, and snap it over your knee. The most important property that this misshapen branch shared with a garden rake was the fact that if you stepped on the curved end, it would cause the straight end to flip up at an extremely high velocity. You would have a brief instant of awareness about what was going to occur, enough time to anticipate the pain but not enough time to prevent it from happening. If you reacted quickly, you could say the "N" part of the word "Noooooooooo!"

And then...impact.

The branch felt like it split Henry's skull in half, though fortunately, it didn't really do that. His bellow of pain caused seven different species of birds to flee their nests. He squeezed his eyes shut and clutched at his forehead with both hands. "Ow!" he said.

"Ow!" he repeated.

"Ow!" he added.

"Ow!" he added again, for clarification.

"Are you okay?" asked Randy.

"I just got hit in the face by a branch!" said Henry.

"I saw."

"It's not funny!"

"I wasn't laughing."

"Are my eyes okay?"

"I think so. Nothing's leaking."

"Are you sure?"

"Open them."

Henry couldn't force himself to open his eyes. His subconscious mind clearly believed that if he lifted his lids, his eyeballs might roll out onto the ground, where they would be eaten by a bear. He knew this was an irrational thought (at least the bear part), but he couldn't get his eyelid muscles to cooperate.

"C'mon, open them," said Randy.

It's okay, Henry assured himself. *They can't roll out onto the ground because they're attached by stalks. Worst-case scenario, they got squished and opening your eyes wouldn't have any additional impact.*

"I think I'm going to take a quick break," said Henry, stepping away.

He'd known that there were trees around. Plenty of them. So it should not have been a surprise when he smacked into one.

At this point, he began to weigh the pros and cons of bursting into tears. He didn't think Max would approve, so that was a negative, and it would be difficult to convince anybody that sitting on the ground and bawling constituted a domination of survival camp. On the other hand, maybe Monica liked sensitive guys.

After a moment of deliberation, he went with the "don't cry like a baby" option. He opened his eyes and was pleased to discover that they remained tightly in their sockets and apparently were still spheres. He was less pleased to see Max staring at him, arms folded, not appearing particularly sympathetic about Henry's level of pain.

"I stepped on a branch," Henry explained.

"I saw."

"I don't think I have a concussion though."

"Good to hear." Max looked at him as if he weren't a very smart person.

All right, Pain, said Henry to his pain, though not out loud. *I'm not going to abandon this challenge because of you. You can just bite me.*

Hahahahahaha! said his pain. *You'll never overcome me! I am your master!*

No, seriously, bite me, said Henry.

Oh, I'll bite you all right. It's going to be a bite that hurts! Because that's what pain does! Rrrarrr!

I really am a geek, Henry thought.

WILDERNESS SURVIVAL TIP!

I hate to be Mr. Obvious, but really, the best way to survive the wilderness is to stay inside. Sure, the outdoors has some cool stuff to see and do, but is it *that* cool?

CHAPTER ELEVEN

Henry and Randy stood there, looking over their completed project. Henry wanted to say something inspiring like "It's not the worst shelter ever made," but that would not be accurate.

Randy sighed. "I'm sure that somebody, somewhere, in a different culture, when humankind was first getting started, built a lamer shelter."

Henry didn't agree with that. He wanted to take pride in their accomplishment, but he'd seen forts made out of couch cushions that would be better equipped to defend them from the elements. Halfway through, Jackie had been instructed to come over and vandalize it. He'd stared at it for a few moments and then decided that there really wasn't anything he could do to make it worse.

No doubt Erik and Stu had made an amazing shelter. Something carved out of marble that they'd found in the woods, with arches, a fountain, and housekeeping service.

"Maybe we could—" Randy began, reaching out to make an adjustment.

"Don't touch it! If you touch it, you'll destroy it! We just need to breathe as gently as possible and hope for the best."

The shelter began to wobble.

"*No*—" Henry whispered.

Wobble. Wobble. Wobble.

"Okay, time's up," Max announced.

Wobble.

Max walked over to their "shelter" and shook his head with the expected amount of disapproval. "Do you two believe that this is an effective shelter?"

"Not really," Henry admitted.

"Because shelters are meant to protect you, not collapse on you and cause your death."

"We know," said Randy.

"If you can't get into your shelter without wearing a full suit of armor, it's not a quality shelter."

"Agreed," said Henry.

Max gave the "shelter" a light tap with his foot. It did not actually explode on impact, but it did instantly break apart into a pile of branches, rocks, and blobs of mud.

"If you'd been inside, you'd be dead," said Max.

"We understand that," said Randy.

"Why would you put skull-crushing rocks at the *top*?"

"They were holding the branches in place," said Henry.

"No, they clearly were not. There's dust rising from your wreckage? Why would there be dust rising from your wreckage? I think you boys successfully made a shelter that was less safe than just dropping the materials on somebody's head!"

"Sorry," said Randy.

"Is that part on *fire*?"

Henry hurriedly stomped on the burning piece with his foot. "No, sir."

"You can't start a fire on purpose, but you can build a shelter that bursts into flames when it falls apart? How is that even possible by any known laws of nature?"

The pile that had formerly been their shelter was sinking into the ground. Henry hoped that Max wouldn't notice.

"It's *sinking*!" said Max. "Why is it sinking? How did you guys find the one piece of unstable ground in these woods?"

"This was a practice shelter," said Randy.

Max massaged his temple as if an alien were trying to break its way out of his head. "I don't even know what to say. This could be what a nervous breakdown feels like. If I didn't spend every waking moment watching for hidden cameras, I'd think I was on a reality show."

A snake slithered out of the wreckage. Henry did not comment on it.

"I've always felt that if you're going to rate something on a scale of one to ten, you should stick to that scale and not try to cheat by saying something is a zero or an eleven or a negative number. But I can't call this thing a one. I just can't. Henry and Randy, your shelter is a zero."

Henry nodded his understanding.

"I hate to belabor the point," said Max, "but if somebody started a magazine called *The World's Most Poorly Constructed Shelters*, this would be the cover story." He pointed to the wreckage. "Not a good shelter, boys. Not a good shelter at all."

They walked through the woods to see Erik and Stu's shelter. "Oh, my God!" Randy exclaimed as it came into view.

"What?" Henry asked.

"That's ten times more mediocre than I would have expected!"

Erik and Stu didn't look all that proud of what they'd built, but at least they hadn't constructed a death trap. It was basically just a line of branches resting along a fallen tree, though the branches had been neatly arranged.

Max tapped the shelter with his toe. It did not collapse, ignite, or sink.

"I'd rate that about a two," said Max. "Congratulations on your victory."

* * *

"Oh, chef!" said Erik, poking his head into the kitchen where Henry and Randy were busy making lunch. They had the window open, but the smell wasn't airing out. "I'd like to start with an appetizer of escargot, extra cheese, extra butter, hold the snail. And then a nice Caesar salad with exactly eleven croutons. For the main course, perhaps a crown roast of lamb with rosemary and oregano, some rice pilaf, and a side of pureed cauliflower. For dessert, I'd like tiramisu with raspberry sauce drizzled on top."

"Me too," said Stu.

"You get hot dogs and a small bag of chips," Henry told them. "And I'm not going to lie. The dogs have some weird things growing on them."

"But if you're nice, we'll cut the green spots off the buns," said Randy. "They're spreading pretty quickly, but if we cut fast, we might be able to catch the decomposition in time."

If you ate each bite with a big mouthful of Coke and swallowed quickly, lunch didn't completely suck.

* * *

"Our next lesson was going to be about canoeing," said Max. "But...I can't do it. Two or three of you would drown. There won't be any canoeing in the Games. Everybody do push-ups instead."

* * *

"Pssst, Randy!"

"What?"

"My hand's caught in my rabbit snare."

"How did that happen?"

"I don't know. Help me get it out."

"Just tug it out."

"I can't. It tightens every time I try. I can't loosen it. I guess that's the sign of a good snare, right?"

"You really can't get your hand out?"

"Shhh! Max will hear you. Hurry. It's cutting off the circulation."

"Okay, okay, let me see it."

"See?"

"Whoa! Whoa! *Whoa*!"

"Shhh!"

"You're going to lose your hand!"

"No, I'm not!"

"Max! We need a knife! Quickly!"

"No, no, it's not that…oh, jeez, I'm feeling dizzy—"

* * *

"Three of the berries on the table in front of you are safe to eat," said Max. "The fourth is not. Jackie, pick the one you think is poisonous."

Jackie frowned as he looked over the selection of berries. "Can I taste them first?"

"Did you really just ask me that?"

"Yeah, what's wrong with…oh, right. Ummmmm." He pointed. "That one."

"The blueberry?"

"Yeah."

"You think blueberries are poisonous?"

"That one might be."

"You do understand that people eat blueberries every single day, right?"

"Maybe I'm misunderstanding the quiz. I thought you poisoned one of these."

"I didn't ask which one was poison*ed*. I asked which one was poison*ous*. If I'm training you to survive out in the wilderness, why would I ask you to identify berries that I had poisoned myself?"

"I can't give you a good answer to that, sir."

"Stu, which one of these berries is not edible?"

Stu pointed. "That one."

"That's the blueberry."

"Oh, sorry. I wasn't paying attention to which one Jackie picked. That's bigger than most blueberries I've seen. How about that one?" He pointed to a small red berry.

"Erik, do you agree?"

Erik leaned down and sniffed the berry. "Yes, sir."

"Randy?"

Randy leaned down and sniffed the berry as well. Then he sniffed the other three.

Max slammed his fist down on the blueberry, squishing it.

"I wasn't picking that!" Randy insisted. "I just like the smell of blueberries!"

"Do you agree with Erik and Stu?"

"Yes."

"Henry?"

Henry picked up the berry and held it up to the sunlight. He didn't know what he was looking for (maybe a skull or Mr. Yuk), but this seemed mildly helpful. He considered squeezing out some juice to see if it sizzled his fingers, then decided against that. He put the berry back on the table.

"Yes, I agree."

Max picked up the berry and popped it into his mouth. He chewed twice and then swallowed.

Everybody stared at him.

"So what do you think?" he asked.

Either Max was conveying the message that they had selected the wrong berry or they'd driven him to suicide. Probably they'd just picked the wrong berry.

"I think you're trying to fake us out," said Erik. "I think you did eat the poison berry, but because it was just one of them and you're a big guy, it won't have any real effect on you. You've probably spent the past couple of decades building up a resistance to—No, I take that back, I think we picked the wrong one."

Max picked up a blackberry. "This is called a pokeweed berry. Ink from this berry was used to write the Constitution of the United States, but it is toxic. Don't eat it."

"Ooooooooohhhhh," they all said as Max massaged his temples much harder than people usually massaged their temples.

* * *

"Henry, where's your fishing hook?" Max asked.

"I'm not sure, sir."

"Why is your face contorted with pain?"

"No reason."

"Why is there a tear trickling down your cheek?"

"The beauty of nature, sir."

"Are you hiding your hand behind your back because you don't want me to know that you somehow jabbed your fishing hook right through it?"

"Yes, sir."

"Show it to me."

Henry hesitated and then held out his injured hand.

"How did you get it to go through *twice*?"

"I'm not sure. It just happened."

* * *

"I caught one! I caught one!" Jackie proudly held up his make-shift fishing pole, from which dangled a very, very, very tiny fish.

"Excellent job," said Max. "Now in the real world, you would throw that back and be a little ashamed to have caught it in the first place, but in a survival situation, you take whatever you can get. So go ahead and clean that fish and we'll cook it tonight by the campfire."

"Yes, sir!"

* * *

"I think Max is really upset," Erik whispered.

"It's not my fault," said Jackie. "I didn't know."

"Soap, Jackie?" asked Erik. "Soap? Really?"

"I've never cleaned a fish! If he wanted me to cut off its head and rip out its guts, he should have said, 'Hey, Jackie, cut off that fish's head and rip out its guts!' There's nothing clean about smooshing your hand through a fish's stomach, right? How am I supposed to know all of these fancy technical terms if he doesn't teach them to us?"

* * *

"Water," said Max, "is the key to all life. I don't care if you have an eighteen-pound ham in your backpack. Without water, you're doomed. But though water is crucial to your survival, you can't always expect to find cool, clear, refreshing water running through a stream. Much of the water you will encounter is laden with bacteria." He held up a gallon jug of water and shook it. "Henry, does this water look safe to you?"

"No, sir," said Henry, even though the water looked perfectly fine.

"Correct. Just because you don't see giant parasites swimming around in there like brine shrimp doesn't mean they aren't there. Water doesn't have to be yellowish or brownish green to be unsafe. This water has literally billions of parasites in there. The horrific things these parasites can do to your insides would make the violence in your precious video games look like—" He glanced at the jug. "This isn't all the way full. Has anybody been drinking this?"

"I got thirsty," Randy admitted. "I didn't know it was plague water."

Max closed his eyes for a very long moment. He opened them, took a deep breath, and continued. "Anyway, when you're drinking water from a potentially unsafe source, it's important to always boil it first to get rid of the bacteria."

"Do we have to boil the water I've already drank?" asked Randy, his voice filled with dread.

"No, Randy. Boiling water while it is inside of your body is not good for your health."

"Am I going to die?"

"I don't know. Probably not."

"Sir?" asked Henry. "I drank the water too."

"Why?"

"Because Randy asked me if I thought it tasted funny. It did, but we figured maybe you just put some weird flavoring in there."

Jackie raised his hand. "Sir? I drank some too. They asked if I could identify the flavor."

"And what did you think it was?"

"Wheatgrass."

Max sighed. "Stu? Erik?"

"I smelled it," said Stu. "Can these parasites get in through your nose?"

"Normally I would say no, but I think you'd find a way to make it happen."

* * *

"That's four feet and eight inches!" Erik announced, letting the tape measure wind back into its container. "Randy wins!"

"He went over the line!" Jackie insisted.

"It's okay if your head goes over the line as long as your feet don't."

"You never said that!"

"That's been the rule from the start."

"Then why did Henry get disqualified?"

"Because he fell over."

"Oh."

"Does anybody else have any left?" Erik asked. "Or is Randy our official distance-puking champion?"

"I've got some more," said Randy. "I think I can beat my own record."

Though Erik ruled that Randy did indeed break his own record, it was a very controversial decision, with Stu and Jackie insisting that one stray chunk did not constitute a distance of four feet and nine and a half inches but that instead, they had to count from where the liquid portion stopped, giving him a rather poor distance of two feet and three inches. Henry and Randy insisted that anything that emerged from his stomach was fair game. Stu and Jackie said that Randy's vote did not count, while Erik said that nobody's vote counted but his own since he was an impartial nonparticipant. Jackie gave it another attempt and was disqualified for spitting rather than regurgitating. Erik's impartial nature was questioned, as was his authority to disqualify the contestants.

They asked Max if he would be a replacement judge, but he declined.

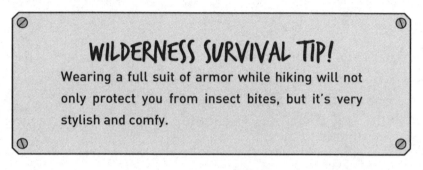

WILDERNESS SURVIVAL TIP!
Wearing a full suit of armor while hiking will not only protect you from insect bites, but it's very stylish and comfy.

CHAPTER TWELVE

They sat around the campfire, roasting marshmallows that would not turn brown no matter how long they kept them in the flames.

"Does anybody know any good campfire songs?" Max asked.

"My chess club has a pretty good theme song," said Stu.

"If you sing about chess, I'll use your hair to start the fire."

"*When you move your pawn, I start to yawn—*" sang Randy.

"How are you in any position to judge chess club?" Stu asked.

"I wasn't judging it. It was the first rhyme I thought of. *When I move my knight, we fight, fight, fight*! See? I wasn't being a jerk about it. *When you move your rook, I…read a book.* No, wait. *When I move my king, I sing, sing, sing*!"

"Stop that immediately," said Max.

"I think my marshmallow is starting to cook," said Jackie.

"That's just an ash that fell on it," Henry noted.

"Oh. Well, I'm going to eat it anyway." Jackie plucked the marshmallow off the end of the stick and then popped it into his mouth. He chewed for a moment. "Muh mah mumma muh mah."

"What?" Henry asked.

"Muh mah mumma muh mah."

"Is that another campfire song?"

"I think he's saying that he can't open his mouth," said Erik. Jackie nodded.

Henry plucked his own marshmallow off the stick and tossed it into the fire, where it continued not to burn.

Max stretched and yawned. "Well, I think it's time to turn in for the night. Tomorrow will be better. It has to be better. It just has to." He stood up.

"Sir?" asked Henry. "I think I'm going to sleep out here again."

"I beg your pardon?"

"It's good for me to be out in the wilderness. I want to try it again."

Max narrowed his eyes. "What's your angle, Henry?"

"Nothing."

"I'd like to sleep outside too," said Randy.

"Me too," said Jackie.

"Yeah, me too," said Erik.

"Pass," said Stu.

Henry's stomach sank. They were going to ruin everything! At the very least, he couldn't let Erik be there if/when Monica showed up. He'd never win her heart if there were more attractive and less clumsy people hanging around.

"Nobody is sleeping outside," said Max. "There'll be plenty of time for that once the Games begin."

Argh! Rats! Shoot! Blast! Dang it! Fudge! Curses! Bummer! thought Henry (again approximately).

Oh, well. He'd make it work. He just had to sneak out after everybody was asleep.

* * *

Henry lay on his fang-covered cot—at least that's what it felt like since unidentified sharp things were poking into his back—waiting for the others to fall asleep. Randy was snoring. The bird chirped every once in a while and Jackie was giving presidential campaign speeches in his sleep. But he wasn't sure about Erik and Stu. He'd just have to wait.

Was it creepy and stalkerish to sneak out of bed and wait outside for Monica to show up? He didn't want to be creepy and stalkerish.

But she'd said that she was going to try to make it out here and that she hoped he'd be around. That meant it wasn't creepy for him to be out there. In fact, for him not to be out there would be rude.

She does have a boyfriend though.

Maybe not.

She does. Accept it, nerd.

Okay, she did have a boyfriend, at least at some point in the recent past. But ultimately, any decisions that Monica chose to make about her romantic life were up to her, and it was not Henry's responsibility to tell her not to trek through the woods at night to meet up with a nerd who wasn't her boyfriend.

Henry didn't want to be the kind of person who would get all snuggly with another guy's girlfriend, but he also didn't think he should carry his sense of social responsibility too far. If she said, "Hey, wanna make out?" should he really be expected to say, "No, no, I cannot do such a thing for that would be wrong!"?

He was pretty sure she wasn't going to invite him to make out.

But if somebody had come up to Henry this morning and said, "Hey, Henry, do you think you'll find yourself taking part in a projectile-vomiting competition today?" he would have said, "Why, no, I think that's quite unlikely." So you never knew what kind of surprises the world had in store.

Chances of Monica inviting him to make out with her

tonight—zero percent. There was a one hundred percent chance of there being a zero percent chance that it would happen.

He listened closely. Erik's breathing seemed to be slow and steady and Stu's wheeze sounded like an unconscious wheeze. He quietly got out of his cot, put on his clothes, and snuck out of the barracks.

* * *

He sat by the extinguished fire in the darkness. He'd brought a flashlight so that he wouldn't twist his ankle in the dark, but he had shut it off once he reached the campfire so he wouldn't alert Max or anybody else.

He looked around for glowing eyes but saw none.

This wasn't so bad. Well, it *was* so bad, but knowing that Monica (might) be on her way made it worth it.

It would be less worth it if all she found was his half-eaten body. Still, he'd accept the risk.

Last time she'd come at one in the morning, so if she kept to that schedule, he had two hours to wait. He probably wouldn't tell her that he'd sat in the dark for two hours waiting for her. She might consider that creepy or stalkerish.

She might not even show.

Right now, she might be laughing to her fellow musical geniuses about how she'd made some dorky, scared guy sit in the dark woods, waiting for her.

"Nobody could be that pathetic!" one of them would say, but Monica would just nod and giggle.

Henry didn't care. He'd risk getting devoured by a wild animal and having people nod and giggle if it meant he might get to spend more time with Monica.

Something moved in the bushes next to him.

It wasn't Monica, unless she'd become very tiny.

Something else moved.

He was surrounded by things that lived in the wilderness. Probably things with claws and teeth and rabies.

He refused to run away screaming.

In fact, he would neither run nor scream.

He was not going to faint. He was not going to whimper. He was not going to gasp.

Okay, some light gasping was fine, but that was it. Let the monsters in the woods scurry around him, searching for his most tender spots. He could handle it. Henry Lambert had been a coward for his entire life—but not tonight.

Not tonight.

As it turned out, he was so brave that he fell asleep despite the danger of spiders crawling into his ears and laying eggs.

When he woke up, Monica was standing over him, shining a flashlight into his face.

She'd brought friends.

WILDERNESS SURVIVAL TIP!
Tree bark is not edible, even with peanut butter.

CHAPTER THIRTEEN

When Monica returned to her living quarters the previous night, Julie, a wide-eyed cello player who was nice enough but a bit too clingy for Monica's taste, had immediately accosted her.

"I was so worried about you!" Julie said.

"I left a note."

"But I didn't know if you'd written it under duress."

"Did you tell anybody I was gone?"

Julie shook her head. "I didn't want to get you in trouble. But I couldn't stop imagining you in somebody's trunk with duct tape over your mouth!"

"Are all cello players this morbid?"

"Yeah, we're pretty dark."

"Well, I appreciate your concern about me being kidnapped by a madman."

"No problem. So where did you go?"

Monica told her. Julia made her swear that she'd bring her along the next time. Monica agreed as long as Julia didn't tell anybody else. Within eight minutes and seventeen seconds (Monica set the timer on her watch), five other girls knew about her adventure and demanded to come along.

"You understand that it's three miles through the woods, right?" Monica asked.

They all said that yes, they understood and that yes, that was totally fine.

"And you understand that I've only seen one of the guys and the rest could be total dog-faces, right?"

The other girls seemed less okay with that.

"It's a survival camp, so they'd be cool guys, right?" Julie asked. "Rugged and stuff?"

"I don't know. I don't think it's a very good survival camp. I make no promises about the quality of the men."

"I'm out," said Tracy, a thin blonde with glasses. "They could be savages."

"And that's bad?" asked Vicki, a thin blonde without glasses.

"It is if they don't wash."

"I'm pretty sure they're not filthy mountain men," said Monica. "But again, I'm not making any promises. I'm just in it for the hike."

"Okay," said Tracy, "I'm back in as long as you promise that they're not filthy mountain men."

"I just said I'm not making any promises!"

"I'm out then."

Everybody else was in.

"Let me make the rules very clear," said Monica. "You have to keep up with me. If you fall into quicksand or something, we will work to save you, but if you just get tired, you're on your own. We leave when I say we're going to leave. And absolutely no whining of any sort. Are you all okay with that?"

"You're kind of bossy," said Tracy.

"I thought you were out."

"I am out, but I'm still allowed to make observations."

"Is everybody else okay with the 'no whining' clause?"

"Is it really three miles?" asked Vicki in a voice that was very close to being whiny, though a skilled attorney could probably successfully plead a case for it not quite crossing the line.

"Yes. Through the woods in the dark. I'd advise against high heels."

* * *

Tracy decided to join the field trip after all but changed her mind after five hundred yards. They walked her back to the living quarters, at which point Tracy decided that she'd go as long as she could hold one of the flashlights.

"Why didn't you just let her hold one of the flashlights?" Vicki asked as they left Tracy behind.

"Who in our group was most likely to drop and break a flashlight?" Monica asked.

"Good point. You think she'll tell?"

"She's probably matured beyond the tattletale stage."

"I'm not so sure."

Monica shrugged. "What are they gonna do to us if she *does* tell?"

"Make us scrub floors."

"I'm not afraid to scrub floors."

"Have you seen the floors in the kitchen?" Vicki shuddered. "I saw some gum under the table and I think it's a brand they don't even make anymore."

"How would you know?"

"I know my gum."

"Did you chew it?"

"No, I didn't chew it. Gross. I sniffed it though. It was from 2005 or 2006."

Monica stopped walking and just stared at her.

"What?" Vicki asked. "Am I not allowed to have skills?"

"Anyway," said Monica, resuming walking, "if we get busted, I'll say that it was my idea, but all of you need to be ready to take some personal responsibility for what we're doing."

* * *

The four remaining girls walked through the woods. Monica took the lead, while Julie walked too closely behind her. Vicki and another girl named Denise followed. Denise was quiet and big-boned; not "big-boned" as an upbeat way of saying "overweight" but rather that she seemed to literally have bones far larger than most girls. Monica would not want to be punched by her.

When they arrived at the campsite, Monica was surprised to discover that Henry was actually there. No sleeping bag this time, and he was fully clothed. He was leaning against a tree, fast asleep. Had he been waiting for her?

She shone her flashlight into his face and he woke up with a start. He looked shocked to see her and then even more shocked to see the other girls.

"Hi," Monica said with a smile.

* * *

For a split second, Henry thought it was a dream. But he did not actually say, "Is this a dream?" because it would have made him sound like a dweeb.

"Hi," he said instead. Definitely better.

"This is Julie, Vicki, and Denise," said Monica, shining her flashlight beam on each of the girls as she introduced them.

"I'm Henry," said Henry, thankful that he was able to say his correct name.

"Did Mr. Roid Rage make you sleep outside again?"

Truth, lie, or somewhere in-between? Henry started to go for somewhere in-between. ("Nah, I just enjoy sleeping out in the fresh air.") But his brain veered away from a possible danger zone at the last instant, and he went with the truth. "Nah, you said you might come back, so I figured I'd just hang out."

"Aw, that's sweet," said Monica, reaching over and brushing at his shoulder. "Ants," she explained.

She's brushing ants off me! I'm the luckiest guy in the world!

"Thanks."

"So is everybody else asleep?"

Henry nodded. "Yeah. I mean, I hope so. Otherwise, they know I'm missing, but they don't care enough to see if I'm okay."

"Well, I'm afraid that we have no other choice but to scare the crap out of them. Passing up an opportunity like that would be unforgivable. Lead us to them."

Henry squished an ant that had crawled behind his ear and stood up. Would this make him a traitor to his gender?

No, they were out in the middle of nowhere and four girls wanted to be led to where the boys were sleeping. *Not* leading them there would make Henry a terrible, terrible human being.

"Let's go," he said. "It's only a couple of minutes away. You'll see the building in a second."

"You said there were five, right?"

"Five counting me. So four."

"Well, then, it couldn't be more perfect. Henry, your job is to sneak in there and make sure everybody is still asleep. If not, you'll signal that to us by coming back outside and telling us that not everybody is still asleep. If they are asleep, we will very carefully creep in there as quietly as possible and everybody will stand at the foot of a bed."

"They're cots."

"Plan doesn't change. Everybody picks a cot. On the count of three, we wave our flashlights, shake the cots, and roar. Everybody can roar, right?"

"Of course we can roar," said Julie.

They reached the building. Henry slowly pushed open the door, expecting it to let out a loud creak because that's what doors did when he wanted them to shut up. But the door opened silently. He stepped into the dark room. Four occupied cots. No motion. Snoring. Everybody was asleep. The evil plan could proceed.

He gestured for the girls to come inside. They turned off their flashlights and walked into the barracks. No floorboards creaked. Nobody sneezed or hiccupped. This was going to be awesome.

Max probably would not appreciate the humor of the prank, but Henry didn't care. Well, he did care but not enough to put a stop to this. Maybe the guys would shriek quietly enough not to wake him up.

Monica took her place in front of Erik's cot. This was the cot that Henry least wanted her to choose, but that was okay. He wasn't going to get jealous yet.

Denise stood at the foot of Randy's cot. Vicki stood at the foot of Stu's cot. Julie stood at the foot of Jackie's cot. She looked a bit disappointed, as if she realized that he was a couple of years younger than her.

Monica put a finger over her lips and then held up three fingers. Then two. Then one. And then—

The sound of the four girls roaring was simultaneously the most hilarious and the most sensual thing Henry had ever heard. Erik, Stu, Randy, and Jackie all cried out in surprise and then there was a trio of crashes as three of the four (not Jackie's) cots collapsed.

The girls cheerfully added to the pandemonium with their own screams.

Jackie scrambled to get out of bed and his own cot collapsed. He knocked over the cot next to him, which knocked over the cot next to it, which unfortunately did not knock over the cot next to it, robbing everybody of the sight of them all going down like dominoes. Jackie fell to the floor. Henry waited a moment to gauge if that was funny or not. (Mild pain would be funny, but moderate to severe would not be.) But when Jackie got up unhurt, Henry deemed it "uproariously funny."

Then suddenly, he wondered what happened to the bird.

But he saw the bird still safely on its cloth on one of the empty cots that hadn't fallen over. So the situation was funny again.

Finally, the screaming stopped, replaced by uncontrollable laughter from everyone. Henry laughed so hard that his sides hurt and tears streamed down his cheeks. He didn't think he'd laughed this hard in his entire life. Even Randy, whose underwear was less presentable than Henry's had been, was cracking up.

"Good one," Erik said. "Good one."

Max burst into the barracks. Henry knew they were making way too much noise not to get caught, so he'd expected this, though the machine gun was somewhat less expected.

"*Who the hell are you?*" Max demanded and then he opened fire into the ceiling.

Everybody screamed and ducked for cover. Monica grabbed Henry's arm and pulled him under a cot.

"Max!" Henry shouted, trying to be heard over the gunfire. "Max! Max! Stop shooting!"

Max did not stop shooting. Pieces of wood fell from the ceiling.

The screams from the girls were not quite as joyous now.

Randy had his hands over his ears and his eyes squeezed tightly shut.

"Max! Please!"

Finally, Max stopped shooting. Or more likely, he ran out of ammunition. He lowered the gun, breathing heavily.

Henry frantically looked around. As far as he could tell, nobody had been hit. All of the girls except Monica were sobbing. Jackie was sobbing too.

"Sir?" Henry called out, not leaving the pseudo safety of the cot. "It was a joke."

"Huh?" Max seemed to realize what he'd done and that the teenaged girls posed no immediate threat.

"They're from the music camp. We were playing a prank."

"Oh." A rather large chunk of the ceiling dropped to the floor, narrowly missing Max's head. He didn't seem to notice it. "That wasn't a smart thing to do."

"I know that now, sir."

Max cleared his throat. "If you are female, vacate these premises and return to your camp of origin."

Nobody moved.

Max tossed his machine gun onto one of the cots and held his hands in the air, palms out. "I'm unarmed. It's okay. I probably shouldn't have opened fire like that."

Monica very cautiously crawled out from underneath the cot. She gestured for the other girls to follow and they all darted out of the barracks without so much as a wave good-bye.

"I'm not opposed to the idea of women sneaking into your sleeping area," Max announced. "But if it ever happens again, try to be more silent."

"We will, sir," said Henry, who was back to not liking survival camp very much.

"Sweep up those wood chips," Max told them. "I'll accept some responsibility for my role in the destruction of the ceiling, so tomorrow we'll work together to repair it."

"Thank you, sir."

Max left, shutting the door behind him. Then he opened the door again, walked back into the barracks, picked up his machine gun from the cot, and left.

"So—" said Erik. "Was that the worst thing to ever happen to us...or the most awesome?"

Nobody slept soundly that night.

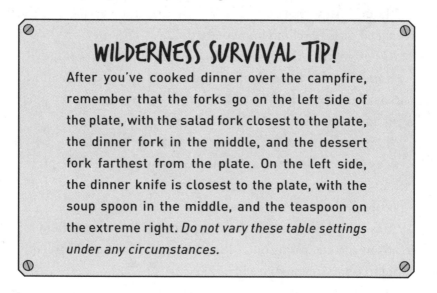

WILDERNESS SURVIVAL TIP!

After you've cooked dinner over the campfire, remember that the forks go on the left side of the plate, with the salad fork closest to the plate, the dinner fork in the middle, and the dessert fork farthest from the plate. On the left side, the dinner knife is closest to the plate, with the soup spoon in the middle, and the teaspoon on the extreme right. *Do not vary these table settings under any circumstances.*

CHAPTER FOURTEEN

Machine gun damage to a ceiling was surprisingly difficult to repair. The boys spent most of their day on the roof, hammering replacement boards over the ones with holes in them. They all kind of wanted to complain that they were here for survival camp, not roof repair camp, but since Max had proven his willingness to use a machine gun, as a group, they felt this would be unwise.

Stu fell off the roof, but he wasn't hurt.

* * *

Lunch might have sucked. They were too hungry to notice.

* * *

Dinner was microwaved pizza. "At least we can't mess that up," said Henry in a statement that he knew would turn out to be ironic even before he finished saying it. As it turned out, there were in fact six different ways that he and Randy were able to mess up the microwave pizza, though only one of them (dropping it) was technically their fault. They did not take responsibility for the indestructible beige substance that was on the microwave tray or the fact that an actual lightning bolt shot out of the microwave at the two-minute mark.

* * *

Of course, the other boys asked how exactly it came to be that Henry snuck into the barracks with a quartet of hot girls. He told the truth. The others explained that for future reference when he had a bunch of girls with him, he should make an effort *not* to create a situation in which Max showed up and ruined everything.

They all snuck out and sat by the unlit campfire, waiting for the girls to show up, but they never did. Henry couldn't blame them.

Day 4: Six Days Before The Games

"Today, we are going to hike," said Max. "It is going to be a long hike and you will not have fond memories of it in your old age. You will each be given two eggs. Those eggs will be your dinner at the end of the hike, so your goal is to protect those eggs during the hike. If you drop them, squish them, lose them, or sit on them, you will go hungry."

The first egg met its demise before Max finished passing out the eggs. Jackie dropped both of his eggs while he was trying to show off his juggling skills, which were not developed at a master level. Most of the other eggs died soon after, though Randy didn't realize that his eggs had met their tragic fate until they took a break and he realized that his backpack was leaking.

Max ate his eggs in front of them. Scrambled.

Day 5: Five Days Before The Games

"It just attacked me!" Henry said.

"A shelter can't attack you," Erik noted.

"It did! I'm not saying that it came alive or anything, but it leaned toward me and scratched me with a branch!"

Max informed them that the Henry/Erik shelter was about eight percent better than the Henry/Randy shelter had been, though he did not seem very impressed by this observation.

Day 6: Four Days Before The Games

"Henry, if you drown in water that doesn't even come up to your waist, I will go after your entire family. I mean it."

Night 6

The guys decided to hike over to the girls' music camp after dark. However, since they did not know how to get there and none of them had superb senses of direction, it did not work out well.

Day 7: Three Days Before The Games

Henry peered through the scope of the rifle, taking careful aim at the aluminum can. That can was toast.

"Remember," said Max, "that rifle has a kick."

In the days before acquiring his astounding new sense of bravery, Henry would have worried about the kick of a rifle. But not anymore. No, not anymore. Rifle kick? What kind of weenie was afraid of a tiny little bump from a rifle?

"Let me make that more clear," said Max. "The position you're holding that rifle in is what I like to call the 'Your Shoulder Isn't Going to Work Anymore After You Pull the Trigger' position.

You may not hear the sounds of breaking bones over the rifle, but that sound will exist. Trust me."

Henry adjusted his position. "How's that?"

"No, do it like I showed you."

Henry had not been paying a whole lot of attention to Max's demonstration. He'd been distracted by thoughts of Monica wearing an impractical outfit that would provide very little defense against the insects. There wasn't much to the attire, but nobody could say it didn't fit well.

Henry adjusted the rifle again. "Is that right?"

"Do you think it's right?"

"I don't know."

"Then let me explain. The way you're holding it is better than if you shoved the butt of the rifle right against your front teeth but not by much."

"I'll hold it differently then."

Henry adjusted the position of the rifle again. He really had no idea what he was doing. He'd been so confident that he'd be able to shoot the can, and now he didn't even care if he hit the can. He just didn't want his arm to come off.

Was a big bruise on your shoulder from a rifle kick the kind of injury that impressed the ladies? Was it closer to "Yeah, babe, I got this scar when a great white shark tried to take a bite out of me, right before I tore its jaws out with my bare hands" or "I forgot to tie my shoes and tripped"?

Probably the latter.

"How about this?" Henry asked.

Max sighed. "Sure, whatever."

Henry took careful aim through the scope. That can was going to have a very bad day. One shot, one dead can, right through the "o" in "Coca" or the "o" in "Cola." He checked that the safety was off just to avoid the embarrassing moment where he squeezed the trigger and nothing happened because the safety was on.

He squeezed the trigger. Nothing happened.

"The safety's on," Max said.

"I just took it off."

"No, you just put it back on."

"Are you sure?"

"Yes. Believe it or not, I do try to give accurate information to teenagers who are holding loaded rifles."

Henry flipped off the safety. He took careful aim again.

Careful aim.

Careful, careful aim.

He would not miss.

Careful…careful…careful—

"*Just shoot something with it!*" Max shouted.

Henry squeezed the trigger. Instead of a direct hit on the aluminum can, he got a direct hit on a clump of dirt about three feet in front of him.

But he'd shot the *crap* out of that dirt. That dirt knew who was boss. It wouldn't be messing with Henry Lambert anytime soon. Oh, yeah.

Day 8: Two Days Before The Games

"I'm bored," said Jackie.

Stu nodded. "Me too."

"Basic survival isn't supposed to be entertaining," said Max. "In a real survival situation, you would be spending every moment thanking God that you're alive. That would entertain you far more than your precious rap music or whatever noise you kids grind into your eardrums these days."

"I'm all about Bruce Springsteen," said Henry, who was not all about Bruce Springsteen but thought Max might be.

"Just watch your trap."

Henry went back to watching his trap. Each of the boys had constructed a box trap up on its side, attached to a rope, with bait underneath, just like in a cartoon. Jackie and Randy's had already collapsed, but Max was making them sit there anyway. By some freakish miracle of physics, Henry's had not yet fallen apart, though he knew that any second could be its last.

They sat there for a few minutes, silently waiting for an unintelligent animal to come by.

"Stu, I think there's a ladybug under yours," said Randy.

"Should I yank the string?" Stu asked Max.

"Is a ladybug your preferred dining choice for this evening?"

"No."

"Then don't yank the string."

"Okay."

"I wasn't saying that you should yank the string," Randy explained. "I just thought you might want to know there was a ladybug under your box."

"Why would he want to know that?" asked Max.

"Why not? I'd want to know. We've already made it clear that nobody's being entertained. We might as well look at a frickin' ladybug. Ladybugs are kind of cool."

"If you're eight," said Stu.

"I guess you've lost your sense of wonder," said Randy. "Sad. So very sad."

"Shhh!" said Henry. A squirrel was climbing down a tree. It reached the bottom, twitched its nose in the cute yet scary way that squirrels do, and then scampered over to Henry's trap.

Would it go for the bait?

Would Henry be able to pull the string at the precise moment?

Would the trap disintegrate?

The squirrel sniffed at the wood, then went inside, and started nibbling at the blob of peanut butter.

Henry tugged the string.

It snapped.

The string was not supposed to snap, since that was what pulled away the stick and caused the box to fall. But this time, Henry's shoddy construction skills worked in his favor and the box fell anyway, trapping the squirrel underneath.

"Good job!" said Max, clapping him on the back hard enough to jostle his lungs. "At least Henry will eat well tonight."

"Eat?"

"Eat."

"I thought this was catch and release?"

"Then apparently you were unconscious during my forty-minute lecture on the importance of being able to catch food. What exactly did you think these traps were for?"

"I knew what the traps were for. I just thought we were being hypothetical."

"Why would we be hypothetical?"

"I don't know. I mean, you don't eat squirrels unless…you know, you're actually starving to death instead of just…you know, *faux* starving to death."

Max just shook his head. "Everybody up."

All of the boys stood up. Max walked over to the box and they followed.

"When you are eating an animal, it is best if you kill it before you put it into your mouth," Max told them. "There are some exceptions, like goldfish or very small frogs, but for the most part, the art of the kill is an important one. The squirrel in this trap will make a fine dinner, but if you try to gnaw on its leg while it's still alive, your face will pay the price."

Henry felt a bit queasy. If this was a movie, he'd be rooting for the squirrel.

"Erik, how do you think we should get the squirrel out?"

"Grab a blanket or a towel, lift up the box, and when he runs out, wrap him up really quick."

"Not bad. But not correct. That tactic could work with slower-moving animals like pugs, but squirrels are much too fast. If you try to catch a squirrel in a blanket, you're almost guaranteed to suffer through wacky madcap antics. Stu?"

"Shoot it through the box?"

"Also a fine suggestion. You're all getting smarter. However, in this case, you'd want to be in an ammunition conservation mind-set and shooting this squirrel would be an unnecessary use of your resources. Jackie?"

"Machete?"

"If you were *extremely* talented with a machete—I mean ninja talented—that might be a good suggestion. Otherwise, no."

"I don't think ninja use machetes, sir."

"Don't ruin my day, Jackie."

"Sorry, sir."

"Randy?"

"I would just come back in a couple of days."

"Really?"

"Yeah, if I hit the point in my life where I was going to eat a squirrel, I probably wouldn't care if it was fresh or not."

"The correct way to dispatch the squirrel," said Max, ignoring Randy's comment, "is to destroy the box while the squirrel is still inside. A few good stomps and your squirrel will be ready to go on the skewer. Henry, step forward."

Henry reluctantly stepped forward.

"This is why I told you to wear a double layer of socks today," said Max. "Now it's important to stomp on the box in the right spot or else your foot could break all the way through, leaving you vulnerable to rabies."

"I'm not going to crush a squirrel to death in a wooden box," said Henry.

"Sure you are. Put your foot up on it."

"I'm really not doing it," said Henry. "I'm sorry. That's not how I was raised."

"You realize that squirrels are a renewable resource, right? I'm not asking you to kill an endangered species. The ecosystem will be just fine without this squirrel."

"I'm not murdering it."

"It's not murder if you eat it, Henry. Unless you're a cannibal and killed a human being. In that case, it would be murder, most definitely. But in this case, with this squirrel, it's hunting."

"I understand your logic. I'm just not killing it."

"Do you think that squirrel likes you? Do you think that squirrel respects you? If you caught a flesh-eating bacteria, that squirrel would laugh his tail off."

"Not gonna kill it."

Max literally looked as if he were about to snarl. "You're the kind of person who would go back in time, have the opportunity to kill Hitler as a baby, and not be able do it. 'Oh, boohoo, I can't kill an innocent little baby!'"

"That's not true. I'd totally kill baby Hitler."

"Pretend the squirrel is Hitler. Do it."

"That's not going to work for me."

Max clawed at his bald head as if trying to rip out his hair. "Where do you think your hamburgers come from?"

"Hopefully not squirrels."

"You disgust me. Go sit down."

Now Henry had to look deep into his soul and decide if he didn't want the squirrel to get stomped or if he just didn't want to be the one to do the actual stomping. He thought it was probably more of the former…but still—

"I'll just hang out here," Henry said.

"Randy, do you want to do what your friend was too cowardly to finish?"

"Not really, sir."

"Jackie?"

"Uhhhhh…yeah, I guess I'll do it." Jackie wiped his hands off on his pants and nervously stood up. "Do I have to look at the guts when I'm done?"

"Look, it's my trap, so I'm going to let him go," said Henry. "If somebody else wants to catch and stomp him, that's fine." He braced himself for the sensation of Max twisting his head off, but Max didn't move. He just stood there, giving Henry a look that showed that he *wanted* to twist Henry's head off but possessed the self-control not to do so.

"Letting him go now," Henry continued. He gently kicked the box onto its side.

The squirrel didn't move.

"You're free, little guy," said Henry, trying to ignore Max's deadly, dagger-filled glare.

The squirrel just sat there, nose twitching.

"C'mon, time to leave. This isn't the safest place for you to be. Go on. Go home to your family."

Still no forward momentum from the squirrel. Max's stare did not diminish in fury.

"So, uh, should I sit back down?" Jackie asked. "Or am I supposed to step on it?"

"Sit back down," said Henry.

Max said nothing.

Jackie hesitated for a moment, wiped his hands off on his pants again, and then sat back down.

Henry gently poked at the squirrel with his toe. "Go on. Go on. Go on."

The squirrel did not heed his advice. What was he supposed to do? Drop-kick it? Was he doing nature a disservice by leaving this squirrel in the gene pool?

"Why don't you give it a name?" asked Max. "Perhaps you could take it home, raise it like your own child, send it to private school."

"C'mon, squirrely squirrel. Time to go."

The squirrel finally scampered off, running back up the tree from where it had come.

Max continued to glare at Henry.

Henry tried to smile. "I did have the one working trap though, right?"

Henry suspected that he would be doing a lot of push-ups that afternoon. His suspicions were correct.

Night 8

"I swear I heard a tuba," said Jackie.

"Are you sure?" asked Erik for the seventeenth time in the past two hours.

"Yes, I know what a tuba sounds like."

"Did you maybe hear it from a different direction? We've gone more than three miles. This isn't right."

"Nothing else sounds like a tuba. And how do you know we've gone more than three miles? Are you Mr. Speedometer?"

"Odometer."

"Are you Mr. Odometer?"

"No, but I know when we've walked three miles."

"How do we know music camp is even still going on?" asked Jackie. "Maybe this was the last day and it was a farewell tuba and that's why we haven't found them."

"I think music camp would have left behind *some* trace of their existence," said Henry.

"I'm bailing on this," said Erik. "He doesn't know where he's going."

"A foghorn sort of sounds like a tuba," said Stu.

"Why would there be a foghorn out here?"

"There wouldn't be. I was just going back to what Jackie said about nothing sounding like a tuba."

"I don't think a tuba sounds anything like a foghorn," said Randy. "I mean, I'm not trying to extend this dumb argument or anything, but I really don't think the two things sound the same."

"It doesn't matter if he heard a tuba, a foghorn, or a million flutes. That doesn't change the fact that there's no music camp around here," said Erik.

"I agree with Erik," said Randy.

"All in favor of turning back, raise your hands," said Henry, who fully expected somebody to tell him that he had no authority to conduct a vote.

Everybody except Jackie raised their hands.

"Fine, be a bunch of babies," said Jackie. "The girls are probably right past those trees right there, but that's okay. Let's turn back."

Another vote was called and they proceeded forward. The girls were not right past those trees.

"Somebody *does* know how to get back, right?" asked Randy.

Day 9: One Day Before The Games

"I have never seen such lethargy!" Max shouted. "You guys are acting like you got ten minutes of sleep last night!"

Technically, it was just over half an hour, but nobody corrected him.

Night 9

"Get a good night's sleep everyone," said Max. "Tomorrow, the Games begin!"

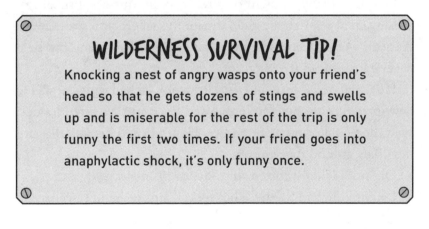

WILDERNESS SURVIVAL TIP!
Knocking a nest of angry wasps onto your friend's head so that he gets dozens of stings and swells up and is miserable for the rest of the trip is only funny the first two times. If your friend goes into anaphylactic shock, it's only funny once.

CHAPTER FIFTEEN

In his dream, Henry held up the glowing crystal Medallion of Amazing Ultimate Victory. Or *was* it a dream? Maybe he really had won the glowing crystal Medallion of Amazing Ultimate Victory.

A stadium filled with tens of thousands of fans was cheering his victory in the Survival Camp Games and fireworks were going off everywhere, including in the stands where the fans were sitting, setting many of them on fire, so yeah, this was probably a dream. He'd read about lucid dreaming, where you were aware that you were asleep and could thus control the dream, but he'd never experienced it.

He wondered if he could fly. Hey, cool, he had wings now! He flew into the air—not too high—and the crowd cheered louder, even the people who were on fire. Henry flexed his muscles and then flew around the stadium.

Oh, no! He'd forgotten to study for his math test!

Oh, no! He had to give a big speech and he hadn't prepared!

Oh, no! He was in his—Actually, he was *proud* to be in his underwear. Look at his muscular body! He would never wear clothing again!

He saw Monica in the stands, using his dream-enhanced UltraMegaVision, and flew over to her. He extended his arms. "Fly with me!"

"Kiss me," she said.

It was dangerous to fly and kiss at the same time. (Many people in other dreams had lost their lives after they had smashed into billboards or mountains.) But Henry didn't care. He leaned his face toward hers. She leaned her face toward his. Millimeters separated their lips and then—

Henry woke up. Monica was not kissing him.

He sighed with disappointment. Then a horde of vampire zombies burst through the wall.

Henry woke up again. Monica was not kissing him this time either. He sighed with disappointment.

"I can't sleep either," said Randy, rolling over on his cot to face him. "I understand that we're not playing for our lives or to earn food for our district or anything like that, but I would *love* for one of us to win this thing."

"I agree," said Henry. "Let's go get some bragging rights."

* * *

"Gentlemen, welcome to the Strongwoods Survival Camp Survival Games." Max was still wearing a camouflage shirt; however, this one was long-sleeved, and he wore a camouflage tie. "This event will show what you are made of. Your strength, endurance, intelligence, and courage will be challenged like never before!"

The five boys stood side by side outside the barracks, arms at their sides, looking ahead, mentally preparing themselves for the ultimate challenge.

"There can be only one victor. You may form alliances, but do so knowing that they will eventually crumble. You have no true friends. The winner of these Games will receive the title of Strongwoods Survival Camp Survival Games winner and also this medal." Max held up a golden medal.

"Is that real gold?" asked Jackie.

Max frowned at him. "Do you *think* it's real gold?"

"I don't know. I guess probably not. What I really meant was…
is that gold plated? With a really thin layer. A thin layer that wasn't
all gold. What I was asking is if there is any gold in that."

"No," Max said. "There is no actual gold in this medal.
You will not be able to sell it on eBay. But if you think that
'Strongwoods Survival Camp Survival Games winner' doesn't
look good on a résumé, then you haven't yet entered the brutal
job market."

"I have a paper route."

"Stop talking, Jackie."

"Yes, sir."

"Forever."

"Yes, sir."

"There are very few rules," Max said. "The boundaries are
clearly marked in orange. If you see an orange flag, orange
paint, or orange tape on a tree, do not go past it or you will be
disqualified."

They'd noticed these boundaries about a mile into the woods
while they'd been wandering around, searching for the music
camp, but they hadn't known what they had meant.

"I have spent most of the night hiding care packages around
the woods. Some contain food. Some contain useful survival
supplies. Some are booby-trapped. But the important ones
contain weapons."

Max reached into his big black bag and took out a pistol.
"This is a paint gun." He pointed it at the side of the barracks
building and fired. The pistol made a *pfffit* sound and a bright
orange mark appeared on the wood. "If you receive three shots
to the torso, you are dead and out of the game. If you receive six

shots to the arms or legs, you are dead. Two extremities shots equal one torso shot, so if you receive one shot to the back and four shots to the leg, you are dead. Everybody clear?"

The boys all nodded.

"In a true survival situation, you would shoot your opponent in the head as much as possible. Unfortunately, these paint guns sting like freaking hell and can cause permanent damage, so head shots are strictly prohibited and will not count."

Henry raised his hand. "Do we get anything to protect our heads, sir?"

"There might be a helmet in one of the care packages," said Max. "Right in there with a rattle and pacifier and diapers."

"So we don't get anything to protect our heads?"

"No. Don't put your face in front of one of the paintball shots and you'll be fine. Now guns are a useful weapon, but that's not all that's available." He took a large hunting knife out of the bag.

Oh, crap, thought Henry. *Head shots are against the rules, but he's going to let us skin each other.*

Max walked over to the building and stabbed it a few times. The blade retracted into the handle and left orange paint marks on the side. "I made these myself. Stab wounds count for fifty percent more than gun wounds, so if you get stabbed twice in the torso, you are dead, and if you get stabbed four times in the extremities, you are dead. One stab to the chest and two stabs to the leg and you're dead. Everybody clear?"

Everybody nodded, even though at least one of them was lying about being clear.

"One of the care packages contains a paint grenade. Use it wisely and you can take out all of your opponents at once."

Henry hoped he found the paint grenade. That would be sweet.

"The Games can last for ten minutes or they can last for four days. It's all up to you. The longer you can survive, the more fun you'll have and the more impressed I will be. Are there any final questions?"

Jackie raised his hand.

"Jackie, I will allow you to ask your question, but I'm going to warn you. If your question annoys me, you're going to take an automatic extremity shot."

Jackie furrowed his brow as he considered that. "I think I'm going to take the risk and ask it anyway, sir."

"Go ahead."

"How will anybody know if we stick to the boundaries?"

"Hidden cameras."

"All over?"

"All over enough. I would advise you not to go past the boundaries."

Henry was pretty sure that Max was bluffing, but he had no reason to test that theory.

"Do I have to get a penalty shot?" asked Jackie.

"No, your question was surprisingly fine. Anybody else?"

Randy raised his hand. "How will we know when people die? Do you have a cannon?"

Max shook his head. "If we had the technology to digitally project the faces of the deceased onto the night sky, believe me, I'd be all over that. The process is that if you are killed, you will return to this spot and I will announce your demise over a megaphone."

Erik raised his hand. "What if I kill somebody but they refuse to admit that they're dead. Can't they just wipe the paint off?"

Max bent down and pulled up his pants leg. There was a faded orange spot on his ankle. "I got hit three years ago. It still hasn't come off all the way."

Henry shifted uncomfortably.

"There are cameras, but do not tarnish the integrity of the honor system. If you are hit, accept it. Cheaters will have their lives ruined. I mean this. You may be thinking, 'Oh, I'll never see Max again after survival camp ends. There's no way he can ruin my life,' but you are wrong. There's one boy, Kirk Maynard, who buried his orange-spotted shirt and pretended to lose it. Every couple of months, I do something to wreck his life. He's twenty-two now. Never got into college. His marriage fell apart after less than a year. He curls into the fetal position every night and cries himself to sleep and I just laugh. Don't cheat."

Henry's stomach was in a knot and he wished he could stop sweating. Insects loved perspiration. He was going to have a really bad experience if there wasn't bug repellent in one of the care packages.

Max pointed to a wooden box that rested on the ground. "This is the first care package," he said, confirming what everybody had pretty much figured out. In fact, Randy had been inching forward just a bit in anticipation of this announcement. "Go for it if you want. Or run. Either way, the Games start in ten…nine…eight—"

Henry could tell that Randy was going to make a run for the care package. Henry was pretty sure that he could outrun his friend, but he couldn't outrun Erik if he also went for it. But if he tackled Erik, then Randy might get the care package, and they could share its contents, unless Randy turned the paint gun on Henry and said, "Our alliance is *over*, dude," and shot him in the torso.

He'd just run. Lay low, let a couple of the others take each other out, hope to find a bow and arrow, and then hope that he was actually good with a bow and arrow, which he probably wasn't since he hadn't been aiming for the target that he hit that one time, but if he aimed for something else besides the person he wanted to hit, his luck might repeat itself.

"Seven...six...five—"

If he won the medal, he'd find Monica on Facebook and she'd know that he was not a total weenie. If he took out Erik in a dramatic manner (which he probably wouldn't) and there really were cameras (which there probably weren't), he'd ask Max if he could have the video (which he probably couldn't) and send it to her.

"Four...three—"

Please don't let him be the first one to die. That would suck so very much.

"Two—"

Henry's heart was racing. It didn't matter that this was a stupid game that probably hadn't been sufficiently play-tested. He was taking this seriously. He'd kill Randy last, but in the end, all of his opponents had to die.

"One—"

He glanced to each side. All four of the other boys were going to run for that box. Maybe they'd all take each other out in the first minute. He was cool with the idea of winning the Games without much of his own participation.

"*Go!*"

Henry raced for the woods. Didn't look back. He could hear a scuffle behind him, but that was fine. Let them fight it out. If he remembered correctly, this strategy had worked for the heroine in *The Hunger Games*, although she did have basic competence on her side.

He ran into the woods. No branches hit him, so he was off to a good start. He'd just run and run until he...tripped.

He pitched forward, threw out his arms to break his fall, and slammed onto the ground.

What a wonderful start. At least no parts of his face seemed to be broken.

The old Henry would have lay there for a while, groaning in pain, but the new Henry got right back up and continued running. It was a wobblier run than before. Still, he kept running.

He ran and ran, now avoiding both branches *and* the act of tripping. He was doing great. He was going to win this thing. Oh, yeah.

He ran until he could run no more, which wasn't all that far, but he was proud for pushing himself to the limit. He leaned against a tree and tried to catch his breath. As he did so, he looked around for a care package.

Nothing.

Could one be buried?

Max hadn't said anything about them being buried and he probably didn't want them going around digging up the whole forest. Still, it was something Henry should have asked about when he had the chance.

Wow, his lungs were really burning. He wondered if Max was watching him on a hidden camera right now, clucking his tongue with disapproval.

Bite me, Max, he thought. *You're going to be putting that medal around my neck.*

Behind him, he suddenly heard a rustling.

Not just a rustling, footsteps.

Not just footsteps, fast footsteps—somebody running.

He looked back and saw Erik, a good distance away but running right at him.

"You're dead, Henry!" Erik shouted.

Henry hoped that he wasn't seeing this correctly, but...yep, Erik had a gun.

WILDERNESS SURVIVAL TIP!

Remember that one tip about wearing the suit of armor? Total lie. Insects can get in through the visor, easily.

CHAPTER SIXTEEN

Henry's first instinct was to climb a tree. Fortunately, he quickly decided that his first instinct was a really dumb one, which would result in him being trapped up in a tree where Erik could shoot him at his leisure.

His second instinct was to run. This was a slightly better instinct, so he followed it.

"You can't outrun me, Henry!" Erik shouted. He was really getting into the role of the menacing villain. "This is the end for you!"

Henry continued to run. *Don't trip. Don't hit a branch. Don't trip. Don't hit a branch. Don't trip. Don't hit a branch.*

He didn't do either of those things. However, he did fail to outrun Erik.

"Stop or I'll shoot!" Erik said, running up right behind him.

Henry stopped so that Erik wouldn't shoot.

"Turn around."

Henry turned around.

"Hands in the air."

Henry put his hands in the air. If he was lucky, Erik would take a cue from other menacing villains and gloat until Henry figured out a clever way to escape.

"Did you get anybody else?" Henry asked, hoping this would lead to eight to ten minutes of gloating.

Erik shook his head. "They all stopped running for the box once they saw I was going for it."

"So why go after me first? The others were closer."

"I didn't want to take out the easiest prey first."

"I wasn't the easiest prey?" That made Henry feel good. "Thanks, Erik. I appreciate that."

Henry looked up, hoping there might be something large up above that he could cause to fall on Erik's head, but no large object was present.

"Any last words?"

"Yes...please don't shoot me."

"That won't work."

"C'mon, Erik. The game just started. I don't want to be the first one out."

"Too bad."

"How about this? I promise I'll stay right here, but you go and hunt down Jackie first and then come back and get me."

"Nope."

"I'm no threat to you. You've got this game won. Everybody knows it. Give me one more chance."

"Not going to happen." Erik pointed the gun at Henry's chest. "Prepare to die."

When the hell was Erik's overconfidence going to transform into his weakness? This was really frustrating.

"How about you just shoot me once? Wing me and then you can finish me off later?"

"Sorry. No."

Erik pulled the trigger.

An orange splotch appeared. Henry winced. It really *did* hurt, even through his shirt.

He turned and ran.

Erik shot him in the back.

Weave, you fool, Henry thought, running through the woods in a zigzag pattern, hoping to dodge the last—

Something hit him in the back.

Maybe it had been a falling acorn.

"That's it," said Erik. "You're dead."

Henry stopped running. His shoulders slumped. "Aw, c'mon, *really*? Why would you do that to me?"

"It's a game. Nothing personal."

"You shot me in the back. That's not cool. You didn't even play with honor."

"Hey, if they'd said that it was against the rules to shoot you in the back, I wouldn't have done it. But it's not, so I did. You're dead. Head back to camp."

"You're a fratchet," said Henry. It was a completely made-up word, but Henry hoped it sounded filthy and venomous.

"Nobody likes a sore loser."

Henry sighed. Erik was right. There was no reason to be a big pouty baby about this, even though he'd never felt a stronger desire to be a big pouty baby in his life.

"*Victory!*" Erik shouted, running off deeper into the woods, waving his gun.

Henry sat down against a tree. He couldn't believe this. Only minutes into the game and he was out. If Monica heard about this, she'd laugh in his face—directly into his face and not in a romantic way or anything.

So now what? Did he just have to hang out with Max until they crowned a winner? Joy.

Maybe he'd propose a new rule: the zombie rule. That would get him back into the game. They wouldn't have to be fast zombies. He'd be okay with just staggering around the woods, hoping somebody came close enough to bite.

He sat there for a while, moping.

Then he got up, brushed himself off, and slowly headed back to camp, resigned to his fate.

* * *

Max sat in his cramped office, munching on a stale power bar. He wished that they really could afford to install cameras in the woods so that he could see what was happening, at least one or two in a central location, but no, Larry refused to buy extra stuff for a camp that was doomed to close after this session.

Oh, well. After he finished up some paperwork, he'd hike out into the woods and try to catch a glimpse of the action. Maybe one of the kids would stun him with some amazing feat of combat dexterity. More likely, one of those fools would accidentally shoot himself in the face, but you never knew—

He looked up from his desk as he heard a car approach. What kind of jackass would show up now just as the Survival Games started? He wasn't expecting any visitors. Maybe it was one of the mothers, deciding that her precious baby couldn't handle the big scary woods after all.

He pushed back his chair, tossed the wrapper of his power bar into the garbage bin, and went outside.

The car parked outside clearly belonged to some rich jerk. Why would you drive a luxury car like that on these kinds of roads? Get a jeep for crying out loud.

He didn't recognize the men who got out; however, they were wearing dark suits and sunglasses, and they clearly believed that they were a very intimidating trio of gentlemen.

They were big guys but not as big as Max.

"May I help you?" he asked as they got out of the car.

"Are you Max?" asked the one who'd been sitting in the back seat. He was the biggest of the three, with a face that looked like he was in his forties but a thick head of black hair, clearly a dye job to hide the gray. Max immediately disliked the creep.

"Yes. And you are?"

"I'm Mr. Grand."

"Do you have a first name?"

"Not to you."

"I'm sorry, but if you're not a superior officer, a judge, or royalty, I prefer to be on a first-name basis with other adults."

Mr. Grand smiled. He had little perfect-white teeth. "All right. It's Peter."

"Please to meet you, Peter. What can I do for you?"

"Is there somewhere we can talk?"

"Sure. Come on in."

He led them into the building. His office was too small to accommodate four people, so he sat down on one of the cafeteria benches. "Have a seat," he said.

"We'll stand," said Mr. Grand.

"Fine," said Max.

"Do you know why we're here?"

"Not a clue."

"I believe you owe us some money."

"I believe you're incorrect. I don't owe you a cent."

Mr. Grand smiled. "Is that so?"

"Unless you're from MasterCard—and I'm not aware of them sending people deep into the woods to collect debts in person—I don't owe you a thing. You've got the wrong guy. Sorry to waste your time."

"Are you not Lester Dexter's partner?"

"Larry Dexter owns this camp. I run it. We're not business partners. I'm his employee." The second these morons left, Max was going to call Larry and give him an explosive earful. He'd had no idea that the camp's financial difficulties were of the "hired goons coming over to collect" variety and it infuriated him that Larry might have misrepresented their relationship apparently to get the heat off himself.

"Hmmmm. That's not how he presented it."

"Again, sorry to waste your time. But not really. You guys look like you've got plenty of time to waste. How long does it take you each morning to fix your hair?"

"Where are the campers?" This was said in a vaguely threatening tone. If Max had any hair on his head, it would have bristled.

"Gone. Camp ended yesterday."

"That's good. So Maxwell—that's your name, right? Maxwell?"

"Call me Maxwell again and see what happens."

Mr. Grand reached inside his suit and took out a gun. A Ruger LCR .38 Special revolver.

"That's a girl gun," said Max as Mr. Grand pointed it at his chest. His bravery was mostly fake now. He did have a knife strapped to his leg, but his nearest gun was locked in his desk drawer. He'd feel much braver if he were wearing his Mylar vest.

"Is it?"

"Yeah."

"Well, then, maybe it will shoot girl bullets that bounce off your chest. I'm a reasonable man, Maxwell. But I need my money—at least a down payment—or this is going to be an unpleasant morning for you."

"How much?"

"Thirty-five thousand."

Max let out a snort of laughter. "Thirty-five grand? You think I've got thirty-five grand lying around here? I don't even have thirty-five bucks."

"That's very unfortunate."

"I'm telling you, Peter, you've been hoodwinked. Larry's probably on his way to the Bahamas right now. You shouldn't have let him out of your sight."

Mr. Grand shrugged. "I'm not worried. Last night, Larry thought he could run away from his debt. He was unsuccessful. So are you saying that I have to kill you too?"

"No, I'm saying that you have to get back in your shiny car and harass somebody who actually owes you money. I'm not part of your criminal underworld or whatever it is. I'll be missed."

"You do have a point," said Mr. Grand. But he didn't put the gun away.

*　*　*

Stupid Erik. Would it really have been such a big deal to let Henry go? Couldn't he have just let him play the game for an hour at least?

Stupid Erik. Stupid, physically adept Erik.

He wondered how Randy was doing. Maybe Randy was walking back to camp too, three orange spots on his torso, head hung in shame. This whole camp was the worst thing they'd ever done and he was never going to let his friend talk him into anything ever again.

Stupid Erik.

What was that?

Something protruded from behind a tree. Henry walked over to check it out and saw that it was a small wooden box. A care package.

Since he was out of the game, it would be against the rules for him to take what was in there, but he could open it just to see what was inside, right?

He crouched down beside the box. It was too small to be a paint-spewing machine gun that could have won him the game, but maybe it was one of those knives. He lifted the lid.

Inside was a comic book. *Spider-Man*.

Henry smiled. It was entertainment in case they had to hide out for a while. Maybe Max wasn't such a bad guy after all.

* * *

"We have a problem here," said Mr. Grand. "I don't think you're a liar. If nothing else, you're more honest than Lester. And looking at the condition of this place, I don't think there's any chance I'm going to collect any money from you."

"I'm a lot of things, but I'm not a liar," said Max, scratching his knee and then inching a bit lower—

"Put your hands in the air please," said Mr. Grand.

"Why?"

"Because I have a gun pointed at you and that is what I'd like you to do."

Max reluctantly put his hands in the air.

"I don't dislike you," said Mr. Grand. "If it were up to me, I wouldn't even ask my men to beat you within an inch of your life before I left. The problem is that whether it's your fault or not, you've become a loose end. And I don't like loose ends."

* * *

Henry, comic book in hand, could see the two buildings up ahead. So at least he wasn't lost. The only thing worse than losing so quickly would be to wander around the woods for a few hours, trying to find his way back to camp.

Would Max shout at him for being such a loser or would he shake his head sadly at him for being such a loser? Henry thought that the odds were sixty-forty in favor of the sad headshake.

Oh, well, he thought. *Might as well get it over with.*

There was a black car parked outside. Henry wondered who that could be. Maybe Max had a secret girlfriend who'd quickly driven there to meet him, thinking that the survivalists would be gone for a while.

Could it be somebody's parents? What if there was some sort of emergency with one of their families?

It was probably no big deal, but Henry jogged toward the building just in case.

* * *

"There are cameras everywhere," said Max.

Mr. Grand shook his head. "No, there aren't."

"You can't get away with just shooting me like this."

"Unfortunately for you, Maxwell, I think that we can. Nice isolated area. Nobody around for miles. I hate to say it, but this is the *perfect* environment in which I could get away with shooting somebody. But I think I can say something that might cheer you up a bit."

"What's that?"

"I'm going to make it quick." He glanced over at the man who stood to his right, a short but bulky guy with a neatly trimmed mustache and beard. "Ethan, if it were your choice, would you make it quick?"

"Not at all."

He glanced at the man to his left, who was a fraction of an inch taller than him. He was clean-shaven, with a deep scar above his right eye. "Chad, would you make it quick?"

"Not a chance."

"So you see, Maxwell, you would be in much worse shape if I left you in the hands of Chad and Ethan. Count your blessings. And now say good-bye."

* * *

Henry reached for the doorknob and then flinched at the sound of a gunshot. That had come from inside the building!

Erik's paint gun hadn't been anywhere near that loud. Had Max lost his already-weak grip on sanity and gone on a shooting spree?

With a sense of intense horror, Henry wondered if their ineptitude had finally been too much for Max to bear. What if he'd seen Henry walking toward the building, already out of the game, and decided to end it all? He and the other boys should have seen this coming and kept Max on twenty-four-hour surveillance.

Three more gunshots, one after the other.

If Max was trying to kill himself, he was very bad at it.

Henry decided that opening the door and strolling into the building would not be the best plan he'd ever formulated. Instead, he hurried over to the window to get a quick peek before he shamelessly fled with his arms flapping in the air. Maybe the car belonged to a friend of Max's and they were shooting up the refrigerator for kicks.

He glanced through the window.

A man lowered a smoking gun as Max dropped to the floor.

At this moment, one of the worst things Henry could do was scream. He instantly realized this and slammed his hands over his mouth to muffle the noise.

It didn't matter, though, because there were two other men in the room and they were both looking right at him.

CHAPTER SIXTEEN AND A HALF

"Rad Rad Roger?"

"Oh, hi, Henry."

"I was refilling my popcorn and I saw you sitting there. What's wrong?"

"Nothing."

"Why are you crying?"

"I'm not."

"Yes, you are."

"I was just reading more of the book, and, you know—"

"What?"

"Max *died*!"

"Oh, yeah. He did. I'm sorry."

"He was the best character! He had all the best lines! Without him, the rest of the book is going to be crap!"

"It's not going to be crap."

"It is! I loved that guy! Who am I supposed to care about now? Stu?"

"Do you need a hug?"

"No."

"Okay. Well, I'm going back into the movie now."

"All right."

"See ya."

"Oh, Henry—"

"Yes?"

"I do need that hug."

"Here you go."

"Thanks. I don't know what came over me."

CHAPTER SEVENTEEN

The men pulled out guns of their own, moving as quickly as a magician making a playing card appear between his fingers. Henry dove to the ground as two more gunshots rang out. The window shattered, raining glass down upon his legs.

Henry decided that it was okay to scream now.

He scooted along the ground until he was away from the window and then got to his feet. Prior to the whole "bullets shattering glass" moment, he'd been willing to believe that this might be a setup by Max to test their abilities to react under pressure, but now he kind of thought that it probably wasn't.

What should he do? What should he do? What should he do? What should he do? What should he do? What should he do?

Had there been a studio audience present (which there wasn't, to the best of his knowledge, though he hadn't quite ruled out the possibility that this was a reality TV show, which would be awesome, way better than people trying to kill him), they would have offered up "*Run!!!*" as a pretty reasonable option. But Henry was a terrible runner. If he fled into the woods, being chased by three physically fit men with guns, he'd be dead. That was simply the natural order of things. Maybe a couple of bullets would miss if they got excited and started shooting before they had a completely clear shot, but still, he had about thirty seconds to live in that scenario.

He had to hide.

There was no place to hide except the barracks, and the barracks were an awful place to hide from gun-toting killers. But what choice did he have? It wasn't as if he could lie in a hammock and casually browse through a brochure promoting the best hiding places of central Strongwoods, weighing the pros and cons of each.

He dashed behind the building, desperately hoping not to trip. This would be a very bad time to trip. If he tripped, he wouldn't even feel sorry for himself. He'd just lie there, getting shot, thinking, "Oh well, that's what I deserve."

Max was dead! He couldn't believe it! Henry had never known anybody who was now dead. Even his ancient cat, Tinkles, was still hanging in there.

Why would anybody want to kill Max? There were plenty of reasons to think that he was an obnoxious jerk, but to kill him? That was way, way excessive.

To be honest, Henry would have expected Max to catch the bullets between his teeth and then spit them back at the shooters. Okay, not honestly. He didn't really believe that. It was time to stop thinking about this kind of stuff and focus on not tripping.

"Hey!" one of the men shouted. It sounded like he was still on the other side of the building and "Hey!" was much better than *bang*! Henry ran across the space between the two buildings, expecting a volley of gunfire to shred him into dog food at some point during those couple of seconds, but thankfully, it didn't happen. He ran behind the barracks and then looped around the building, stopping quickly to peek out front.

No sign of the maniacs.

He hurriedly opened the door to the barracks, slipped inside, and closed the door behind him.

He breathed a deep sigh of relief. He was safe.

No, he was anything *but* safe. With a whole vast, expansive, tree-filled forest at his disposal, he'd shut himself in the barracks! He'd done exactly what he sat on the couch and yelled at people in movies for doing. This was worse than if he'd tripped. Where was he going to hide? Under a cot? What kind of conversation did he think they would have?

SCARY GUN MAN #1: Gosh, I have no idea where that rascal might've gone! He's outwitted us but good!

SCARY GUN MAN #2: I'm so tired of these clever folks making us look like common dullards! Maybe we should check that building right there.

SCARY GUN MAN #1: You haven't got the sense that the Lord gave a headless donkey. Do you think he's just sitting in there, eating a bowl of grits? I should knock you on your fool head for saying that.

SCARY GUN MAN #2: Why do you always ridicule me so? I was just thinking that it would take maybe nine or ten seconds—eleven at the most—to take a look in there. I wasn't suggesting that it become the focal point of our pursuit, just that—

SCARY GUN MAN #1: Hush your mouth before more ignorance spews forth from it. He isn't in that building and we aren't wasting nine to eleven seconds proving a theory that we already know to be incorrect. Give me your head so I can whup it.

SCARY GUN MAN #2: Ow! It wasn't necessary to whup me that hard! That hurt more than the corn on my little toe!

SCARY GUN MAN #1: Shush it. Now let's go find that rapscallion and don't let me hear your flapping lips speak any more stuff that doesn't have any smarts in it.

That scenario was unlikely.

And yes, he was going to have to hide under a cot.

* * *

"What do you think you're doing?" Mr. Grand demanded.

"A kid saw us!" said Ethan.

"That doesn't mean you should start shooting out windows! Show some common sense for crying out loud! I don't pay you to act like psychos!"

Mr. Grand tapped Max's body with his shoe to make sure he was dead, not that there was any real doubt about the matter. There was a time when he would have felt bad about having to kill an innocent man like this—somebody who didn't turn into a sobbing baby, blubbering and begging for mercy. Those days were long gone. Baldy shouldn't have mouthed off to him.

"Go get the kid," he told Ethan and Chad, dismissing them with a wave.

"Kill him?" Chad asked.

Mr. Grand shook his head. "No, I want to talk to him."

"But he saw us."

"Are you questioning me? Shoot him in the leg if you have to, but bring him back alive. Go!"

Ethan and Chad hurried out of the building. The guys were good muscle, but Mr. Grand couldn't believe how dense they were sometimes. You catch the kid, find out what he knows, and *then* kill him. This wasn't rocket science.

It had been brain surgery once, though not surgery with the intention of *fixing* the brain. That one got out of hand. Everybody had felt kind of awkward during the cleanup. He probably wouldn't let that happen again.

* * *

Henry lay under the farthest cot, wishing he had a better plan than hiding under a cot. They'd see him for sure. In fact, it might be better to just greet them in the middle of the room, hands in the air, a friendly and nonthreatening smile on his face.

They had no reason to kill him, right?

Sure, there was the whole "witnessing a murder" issue, but they could work that out. They might think that a sixteen-year-old who was dumb enough to hide under a cot in the next building would be an unreliable witness in front of a jury.

What would a real action hero do in this situation? Besides already know martial arts?

Maybe he could smack them with a cot.

The door swung open. Henry's entire body tightened. He could feel internal organs that he didn't even know he had constricting.

He could see the feet of one of the men stepping into the barracks. Just one man. That was good. If they'd split up, then they didn't know for sure where he was.

The man walked farther inside, the floor creaking with each step. Henry did not recall the floorboards creaking any of the other dozens of times he'd heard people walking across them. Apparently, those jerk floorboards just wanted to make the experience scarier.

"Hello?" the man said.

Henry wisely did not respond.

"Helloooooo? Anyone in here?" There was a mocking, cruel tone to the man's voice, but Henry wasn't sure if he'd actually been seen or not. Best to just remain perfectly still.

He felt a cough coming on…and a sneeze…and a hiccup. His body was really being a creep right now.

"Hellooooooo? I understand that there's a naughty little boy hiding in here."

Naughty little boy? Seriously? Henry knew that he looked young for his age, but how old did this guy think he was?

The urge to sneeze intensified, probably from the dust underneath the cot. The urge to cough also got worse. The urge to hiccup mercifully faded, which was nice because it would really suck to die because of an uncontrollable hiccup.

And now he was getting a leg cramp. Next, an alien would probably start to burst out of his chest.

"Whatever shall I do?" asked the man. "I just don't know where that naughty little boy might be hiding. Perhaps I should start shooting the beds one by one and see what's underneath?"

At this point, Henry had a pretty good idea that the man knew where he was hiding. He went ahead and succumbed to the sneeze, which was such a violent sneeze that he smacked his forehead on the wooden frame of the underside of the cot. Nice. Apparently, he'd been in danger of not feeling enough like an idiot.

Now that he was in a situation where he really *might* die, Henry wished he hadn't spent so much of his life thinking that he was going to die in nondangerous situations. He could have swam in the ocean. It would've been fine. No sharks would have bitten him in half. He could have ridden that roller coaster. It wouldn't have fallen off the track during the loop-de-loop and dropped onto another coaster that was following too close behind because the ride attendant wasn't paying attention to what he was doing. He could have pet that—Well, no, the poodle was vicious—

"Come out of there," said the man.

Coming out of his hiding spot seemed like a truly terrible idea, but it was either that or kick the cot from beneath, sending it flying across the room and into the man's face.

Henry slid out from underneath the cot. He wasn't going to

start pleading for his life quite yet. He'd be polite and yet convey the message that he really did not want this man to shoot him.

"Stand up," the man said. He raised his voice. "I've got him!"

"I didn't see anything," Henry said, slowly and carefully standing up.

"Nothing? You sure? Because there was a big bloody corpse right there. Hard to miss." The man grinned. Henry wondered how he got that scar over his eye. Probably a broken-bottle fight. "Hands in the air."

Henry put his hands in the air.

"You packing?" the man asked.

"What?"

"I asked if you were carrying a gun."

"Oh...no."

"Too bad for you. Guns are handy. Anyway, don't freak out on us or anything. We just want to ask you some questions. Nobody's going to hurt you."

The lie could not have been more obvious if his nose had suddenly shot forward eighty feet, stretching out long enough to break through the back wall. They were absolutely going to hurt him.

"I won't say anything," Henry promised. "Not a word."

"Good. That will make things easier."

"I mean it."

"And I believe you. It's nice that you're so willing to cooperate with us."

The man who'd killed Max stepped through the doorway, still holding his gun. Unlike the other guy, this man was not grinning.

"You've created a bit of a problem for us," he said.

Henry shook his head. "I'm not a problem for anybody. I'm no threat. Believe me, I'm really, really lame. You have nothing to worry about. Honestly, having me testify against you would probably *improve* your case because I'm so...you know, bumbling."

"Don't talk yet. Ethan, bring him over to the other place so we can sort this mess out."

The man walked out of the building. Ethan strode toward Henry with the confidence of somebody who knew that this skinny kid wasn't going to cause him any trouble. His confidence was justified. He got behind Henry and twisted his arm up behind his back. Henry cried out in pain but didn't struggle as Ethan quickly walked him out of the barracks and into the other building.

Henry squeezed his eyes shut as soon as he caught a glimpse of Max's dead body on the floor. He knew that he should keep his eyes wide open, searching for any possible opportunity for escape, but he just couldn't look.

"Chad, keep an eye out for more of them," he heard the man who'd shot Max say. "Ethan, what are you doing? Having a wrestling match? Sit him down."

Ethan jerked Henry's arm up, sending a bolt of pain through the entire right side of his body, and then slammed Henry onto the bench.

"Open your eyes," said the man.

Henry reluctantly opened his eyes but turned away from Max.

"I don't like to kill kids," the man said. "But you're old enough that I won't think of you as a kid, so make no mistake, if you don't answer my questions, you'll end up like your counselor." He gestured toward Max with his thumb. "How many more of you are here?"

"None," said Henry. He was more terrified than he'd been in his entire life, but no matter how scared he was, nothing would make him say something to cause these men to send a hunting party after his friends.

"None?"

"Just me." Why would there only be one kid at the camp? Henry thought quickly. "Just me and my uncle Max."

The man stroked his chin. "Hmmmm. What's your name?"

"Henry." No reason to lie about that at least.

"I had a stuffed walrus named Henry once. Lost my temper over something or other and ripped him apart, tusk to tail."

Henry wasn't sure how he was supposed to respond to this anecdote, so he said nothing.

"Let me clarify this for you, Henry. If you tell me who else might be out there, we'll round them up, ask them a couple of questions, and then everybody can go on their way. If you don't answer my question honestly and we see your friends, I promise you we'll shoot them on sight. Is that what you want?"

Though Henry had done nothing to give the impression that he was intelligent, he couldn't help but object to being treated like he was stupid. If you were trying to hide a murder, you didn't round up people in the area and ask them questions.

"It's just me," Henry insisted.

Ethan snickered. "Then why did five of the cots have people's bags on them?"

It was, Henry had to admit, a superb question. "They're on a field trip."

"To where?"

"An indoor shooting range."

"*Bzzzz!* Sorry, Henry. That doesn't match what your uncle Max told me. He said camp was out. I think both of you were trying to mislead me."

"What I meant was—"

The man held up his palm. "Don't talk. Tell me...have you ever heard of somebody named Mr. Grand?"

"No."

"Well, you wouldn't have, since I assume you're not familiar with the players in the criminal underworld. But Mr. Grand is me. If I didn't want to preserve your youthful innocence for a few more seconds, I could tell you some of the things I've done. For simplicity's sake, let's just say that I don't mind getting my hands messy. To be more descriptive would be impolite."

Ethan snickered again. Mr. Grand glared at him and then continued. "What I'd like you to take from this conversation, Henry, is the observation that I am a very bad person who has done a great many bad things. Our whole problem is that you've seen me do one of those bad things, which is information we can't let you give to the police, and yet I've just told you my real name. How does that make you feel, Henry?"

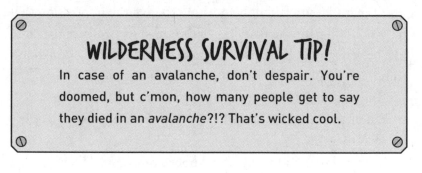

WILDERNESS SURVIVAL TIP!

In case of an avalanche, don't despair. You're doomed, but c'mon, how many people get to say they died in an *avalanche*?!? That's wicked cool.

CHAPTER EIGHTEEN

Henry's stomach lurched and his last meal, which until now had done a surprisingly good job of remaining inside his body, ceased being a victim of the digestive process and shot back up into his throat. He slammed his hand over his mouth and instinctively bolted for the bathroom, even though there was no bathroom in this building.

Ethan howled with laughter.

Henry's vision blurred and he realized that it was blind luck that kept him from slipping on the blood, or worse, tripping over Max's dead body. He stumbled forward, desperately trying to keep from spewing all over the place. He wasn't sure how that would make his situation worse, but he wanted to avoid the humiliation if at all possible.

Then a very clear thought: *Work with this!* They hadn't shot him and yet he was up and running around when he wasn't supposed to be. If they spent a few more seconds thinking he was a laughable buffoon, he could get into Max's office and crash through the window!

He bolted for Max's office, ran inside, slammed the door behind him, and locked it.

It had worked! It had actually worked! He was just like an action hero!

Then he finally threw up, which made him feel less like an action hero.

He wiped his mouth with the back of his hand and quickly glanced around the tiny office. The first detail that he noticed— and it was an important one—was that there was not a window. Somebody on the other side began to violently pound on the door. It was probably not the cavalry. Since the building itself seemed to be on the verge of falling apart, Henry didn't think the door was going to provide much protection against large men with guns.

Henry frantically looked around for something that could help him, such as the entrance to a bomb shelter. You'd think that a guy as paranoid as Max would at least have a panic room, but nope, it seemed like a regular office.

Where were the machine guns displayed on the wall? Where was the pile of emergency dynamite? Where was the ceremonial samurai sword? Where was the tank? This was all just papers and stuff.

He opened one of the desk drawers. Inside were three bottles of whiskey but no weapons. If they weren't in here, then the big black bag of weapons must be stored in the closet next to the kitchen, which didn't do Henry a whole lot of good right now.

The pounding on the door turned into a kicking and the door shook on its rusty hinges. That thing was going to burst open any moment now, and in the battle of Frightened Teenaged Kid with a Whiskey Bottle v. Two or Three Big Men with Firearms, Henry thought that he had a good chance of losing.

The only thing that even looked like a weapon was a joke grenade on the corner of the desk. A tag with the number three was attached to the pin, and a sign read, *Please Take a Number*. Henry thought his dad had the same gag in his office.

Henry knew that Max, may he rest in peace, would have wanted him to turn a phony grenade to his advantage.

He grabbed the grenade off the desk and yanked off the three just as the door flew open, coming half off its hinges. Henry suddenly had two guns pointed at him by two extremely angry looking men, but he raised the hand with the grenade and tried not to panic.

"Get out of my way!" he shouted. He felt that harsh profanity would be appropriate here but worried that he might not be able to pull off the necessary attitude, so he left it out. "Get out of my way or I'll blow us all to bits!" Without even waiting to see if his bluff was going to work, Henry strode for the doorway, praying that they would step out of his way.

They did. Mr. Grand and Ethan didn't give him a lot of clearance, but Henry was able to push past them, trying to hold the grenade like he meant it.

"Don't mess with me!" he warned them, moving toward the main door to the building. "I'll blow us all up! I'll do it!"

Ethan cackled with laughter. That was not a good sign.

"You don't even know how a fragmentation grenade works!" he said. "You don't blow people up with it. Don't they teach you anything at this camp? Man, if I paid to come here, I'd demand my money back."

Henry tossed the grenade at him.

Ethan's smile disappeared like…well, like somebody had tossed a grenade at him. His gun fell out of his hand as he scrambled back out of the way. For part of a fraction of a split second, Henry thought about going for the gun, but he'd never be able to grab it before Ethan did, so instead, he rushed for the exit.

He made it.

He sprinted for the woods.

Made it there too.

A gunshot rang out, and though he didn't feel a bullet whoosh past his ear, he thought it came pretty close. He kept running, pumping his legs as fast as he possibly could.

Another gunshot. A leaf popped off a tree in front of him, but that might have been a coincidence.

Don't trip, don't trip, don't trip, don't trip—

Don't hit a branch, don't hit a branch, don't hit a branch—

Don't die of a heart attack, don't die of a heart attack, don't die of a heart attack—

A third gunshot, but this one sounded a bit farther away. Maybe the shooter wasn't actually chasing him. You couldn't shoot very well when you were running.

If Henry didn't trip, hit a branch, or die of a heart attack, he might actually be okay! The trees were definitely too thick now for somebody to get a good shot. In the face of mortal danger, his running abilities were way better than he ever imagined possible.

A true action star would turn around and shout something clever, but Henry felt it was best to skip that step. He kept running.

No more gunshots.

He wondered how mad they were about the fake grenade. Probably *very*.

He wanted to quickly glance over his shoulder to see if anybody was chasing after him, but he didn't want to give them an unfair advantage by falling and breaking his legs, so he just kept running and running and running.

He wasn't sure how long he'd been running before, completely exhausted, he had to stop. Maybe as long as ten minutes but probably something lamer like five. He stopped, braced himself against a tree, and tried to catch his breath.

Henry looked back. There was no evidence that anybody was pursuing him.

He was safe. He'd actually gotten out of that situation without Batman breaking through a window and rescuing him. If Max really did have hidden cameras set up, that would be the most awesome thing imaginable.

Then Henry felt guilty for thinking about the awesomeness of his accomplishment when Max was dead. Max didn't deserve to be shot in the chest. He was strict and insane but well meaning, and given the opportunity, Henry might even try to avenge his death. Not one of those deals where you spend your entire life searching for the target of your revenge at the total expense of anything resembling a social life, but if convenient vengeance ever presented itself, he'd definitely take it.

At least these ridiculous vengeance thoughts were keeping him from focusing on how frightened he still was.

Well, no, he was still focusing on that pretty well.

They could still be coming after him.

He thought that he could probably find the dirt road that had taken him to camp in the first place, but it had been fifteen miles long. Fifteen miles before he could make it to a road that might contain actual traffic to flag down for help.

A much better option would be to find the music camp. Except that he could wander around forever looking for it. Not literally forever. They'd eventually find his shriveled, dehydrated body lying on the ground somewhere. And then they'd say, "Oh, look, the music camp was just past that tree. How ironic."

So getting help was going to be a nightmare. But really, that wasn't his top priority right now. He had to warn the others. He couldn't let them go back to the building.

Somebody moved maybe ten feet away.

Henry's stomach lurched. How had they gotten so close?

More movement. Somebody running from the cover of a large tree to the cover of another large tree.

"Who's there?" Henry demanded. No way could Ethan or Mr. Grand have followed him that closely without him hearing them. Had he been so unfortunate as to run in the same direction that the third guy had been searching?

Erik stepped out from behind the tree, pointing his paint gun at Henry. The paint gun looked significantly less scary now that he'd encountered the real thing. Henry breathed a sigh of relief. "Oh, thank God."

Erik shot him in the chest. Relieved or not, it still stung like crazy.

Erik shot him three more times as he walked over to him. Henry tried to block one of the hits with his palm, which hurt much worse than just taking the shot to the chest.

"Erik, listen to me," said Henry, wiping his orange palm off on his shirt.

"No, you're cheating."

"No, no, it's not like that."

Erik grabbed Henry by the back of the neck and pushed him forward.

"Erik, listen. Max is dead!"

"Uh-huh. Right."

"He's dead! Didn't you hear the shots?"

"Yeah."

"That was Max being shot to death! I saw his body!"

"Stop being such a loser."

"I'm serious! These three men showed up at camp and they murdered Max!"

"You just don't want him to know you got out first." Erik

continued to push Henry forward. Wow. The guy was even stronger than Henry had expected. Under different circumstances, Henry would have been impressed and perhaps even complimentary.

"I'm not lying! I wouldn't lie about that! Can't you hear me spazzing out? Would I spaz out like this if I wasn't telling the truth?"

"Shut up."

"You're going to get us killed!"

"You're already dead. I thought you were cool, but you're a cheating weasel. Max is gonna throw a fit when he finds out."

"Corpses don't throw fits!"

"Just let it drop," said Erik. "I'm taking you back to camp, so you'd better deal with it."

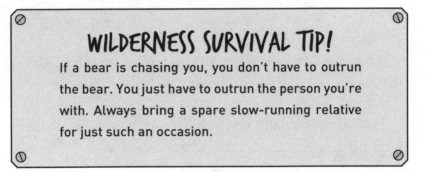

WILDERNESS SURVIVAL TIP!

If a bear is chasing you, you don't have to outrun the bear. You just have to outrun the person you're with. Always bring a spare slow-running relative for just such an occasion.

CHAPTER NINETEEN

Randy and Stu walked through the woods together. They'd both run in the same direction after Erik got to the box first, and since neither of them had acquired paint weapons yet, they figured they might as well have somebody to talk to while they searched.

"Did you hear that?" Randy asked.

"You mean that really loud gunshot that anybody would have heard?"

"Yeah, that." Randy was very good at ignoring sarcasm. A couple more shots followed. "What was that?"

"A gun maybe?"

"I mean, do you think Max lost his mind and started shooting up the place?"

"Maybe they came from the music camp."

"Why would there be gunshots coming from the music camp?"

"That stuff is competitive. You don't know what it's like. A piccolo player misses out on first chair and things get ugly."

"That's not it. It came from our place."

"I guess you're a human GPS."

"Do you really not know how to directionalize sound?" Randy asked. "It obviously came from our place. And being a human GPS would not mean that you could tell where sounds came from."

"Well, 'directionalize' isn't a word."

"Yes, it is."

"If it is a word, it would mean to be able to make sound go in a certain direction, not to tell which direction sound came from. So it's either a fake word or you're using it wrong."

"Maybe we should walk separately," Randy suggested.

"That's a good idea," said Stu.

They continued to walk together. Randy noticed a small box resting next to a tree and tried to be casual about it. "I'm just going to stop and let you go on ahead."

Stu regarded him with great suspicion. "Why?"

"Because we just established that we're annoying each other."

"What did you see?"

"Nothing."

"So let's walk together for another few minutes."

"I have to tie my shoe."

"I'll wait. I needed to tie my own shoe anyway."

They both bent down and pretended to tie their shoes.

"We're not doing each other any good hanging out together," said Randy. "You go that way. I'll go this way and we'll meet up again when we're ready to kill each other."

"You see a care package, don't you?"

"Nope."

"Where is it?" Stu began turning his head in all directions, including a couple of directions that seemed like a head shouldn't swivel without the assistance of a demonic possession.

"I didn't see one."

"You're full of beans."

"Beans?"

"Yeah."

"I've never heard that expression."

"Everybody uses it. You need to get with the times."

"I'll say it every day if you just leave me alone."

"I'd have no way to verify that you said it."

"Look, Stu, why don't you just—" Randy finished his sentence with an expression that he *knew* was in heavy rotation.

"That's classy."

"The Survival Games aren't about being classy."

Stu's eyes widened—again, in a manner that seemed enhanced by spirits of darkness—and he pointed. "That's what you saw! You liar!"

Stu ran for the package.

Randy would have tried to stop him, but he'd been looking at a different box. He ran for his own package, hoping his contained a paint grenade and that Stu's contained a paint turd. But his was about the size of a shoebox and Stu's was about the size of an Xbox box, so he worried that Stu might have the advantage.

Randy tried to lift the lid, but it was nailed shut.

He looked over and saw Stu lift his lid without any problem. How was *that* fair?

Stu reached into his box and removed what was inside. "Another box?" he exclaimed. "How is that fair?"

Randy didn't have any tools with which to pry open a wooden box lid, so he began to kick the box. He assumed that if there were a squirrel inside, he'd have heard it scurrying around in there.

Stu opened the lid to the second box. "Another box!"

Randy's box wasn't breaking. He picked it up and slammed it against a tree. The tree received a much bigger dent than the box, even though they were both wood.

"Another box!" said Stu.

Randy slammed the box against the tree a few more times, but that wasn't doing any good, so he dropped the box on the ground and began to jump on it. That worked. The wood cracked immediately, and after the third jump he was able to see what was inside—another box.

He tossed aside the pieces of the first box, picked up the second box, and swung it against the tree. This turned out to be unnecessary, since the lid hadn't been nailed shut and a long plastic knife fell to the ground.

Filled with a gleeful sense of approaching victory, Randy snatched up the knife and turned toward his opponent. Stu had finally opened the last box and held up his own identical plastic knife.

"You're not allowed to stab me in the face," said Stu.

"I know that."

"Just making sure. You also can't stab me in the ear."

"I wasn't going to."

"No head stabs at all. That's what Max said."

"I was there. You don't need to repeat the rules."

"Just making sure."

The boys began to circle each other, fierce warriors about to do battle.

"I vote we test these first," said Stu. "They're only plastic, but if the blade is stuck, one of us could get hurt."

"That makes sense."

"Just test it on your arm to make sure."

Randy jabbed his arm with the blade. It retracted all the way into the handle, leaving behind an orange mark. "Mine's fine. Test yours."

"That counts as a stab," said Stu. "Max never said you couldn't stab yourself. You've got one injury."

Randy felt like this was something they could argue about for the next 857 hours, so he decided to let it drop. Instead, he charged at Stu, tackling him to the ground.

He stabbed Stu in the chest.

Stu stabbed him back.

He stabbed Stu again.

Stu stabbed him back.

More gunshots rang out.

They stopped stabbing each other for a moment.

"What do you think's going on?" Randy asked.

"I'm telling you…Max is hallucinating communists."

"Maybe we should go back and make sure everything's okay."

"Maybe you should—" Stu stabbed Randy in the chest "—go back and tell him you're dead."

"You suck, Stu."

"Apparently not."

Randy got up and brushed himself off. Great. He'd lost to Stu. At least if he'd lost to Erik, people would say, "Well, it's a shame that you lost, but Erik is pretty awesome, so if you had to lose to anybody, it might as well be the strongest and fastest of you all." And if he'd lost to Henry, he could at least say that he'd lost to his best friend. And if he'd lost to Jackie, well, Jackie would be really happy that he'd won the fight, and Randy could have pretended that he'd let Jackie win in an effort to help with his self-esteem issues. But losing to Stu was pure suck.

"A good sport would help me up," said Stu.

Randy wasn't feeling like a good sport, but he helped Stu up anyway. He half-expected Stu to try to yank him back to the ground so he could get in a hearty chuckle, but Stu probably realized that his twig arms weren't up to the task, so he merely said, "Thanks."

"I hope you feel good about a dirty win," said Randy.

"It feels better than a clean win actually," said Stu. "I'm kind of uncomfortable with what that says about me."

"Well, have a good game. Maybe somebody else has died already and I'm not the first one out."

"Max hasn't announced anything over the megaphone, so you may be in luck. Of course, if he's shooting at nightmares, he'd be too distracted to keep us updated."

"Maybe we should go back and see if anything's wrong."

"Sure, if a whack nut is shooting randomly, that's where I want to be."

"What if he hit somebody?"

Stu laughed. "C'mon, Randy, you're way too uptight. Nobody's hurt. Max is out there shooting blanks to rev us up. Here, I'll walk you back as my dead prisoner."

* * *

Jackie sat comfortably in a tree. This comic book he'd found in a care package was fantastic.

* * *

"So what do we do?" Ethan asked.

"First of all," said Mr. Grand, "we ask ourselves how that little twerp got away from us."

Ethan shrugged. "He ran to throw up, locked himself in the office, and then tossed a fake grenade at us."

"Do you really believe that I was asking for a literal answer? Seriously?"

Chad walked back into the building. "What happened? I heard shots."

"The kid got away."

"How?"

Mr. Grand ignored the question. "Did you find any more?"

"Nah, they could be hiding anywhere in the woods, I guess, but I didn't see any."

"There are probably four more," said Ethan.

"Ouch. Are we calling for backup?"

"I hate the idea of getting backup for a few bratty kids...but yes, that's what we're going to do. It will take a while for a team to get out here and I'd rather pay them to waste their time than have this situation get out of control."

Ethan and Chad nodded. Ethan hoped that Foamer would be part of the team. It amused him to no end to watch that guy go all rabid-dog on a victim.

"Get the body into the trunk and clean up the mess," said Mr. Grand. "I'll keep an eye out on the perimeter while I make the call."

"Shouldn't I hunt for them some more?" Chad asked.

Mr. Grand shook his head. "Waste of time. They could be anywhere."

"All right. Maybe we'll get lucky and they'll just walk right back here."

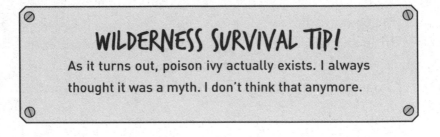

WILDERNESS SURVIVAL TIP!

As it turns out, poison ivy actually exists. I always thought it was a myth. I don't think that anymore.

CHAPTER TWENTY

"You have to listen to me," Henry insisted. "You're gonna get us killed!"

"Enough!" said Erik.

"They had me at gunpoint! I faked them out with a phony grenade and then ran out the door!"

"Oh, yeah? Did you knock them all unconscious with your amazing kung fu action too?"

"Why would I lie about this?"

"Millions of reasons. I don't believe you and I'm not going to believe you, so stop talking! By the way, you reek."

"That's because I threw up! I puked when they had me at gunpoint!"

Erik stopped. "Let me see your mouth."

Henry opened his mouth. Erik ran his finger over the side of Henry's mouth and then sniffed it. "You *did* puke."

"I told you!"

"I don't believe you, but for now, we'll pretend that I do."

"Thanks," said Henry.

"So what should we do?" Erik asked.

Henry had been hoping that Erik would come up with a detailed and brilliant plan immediately after acknowledging that Henry might have been telling the truth, but he didn't want to say, "Duhhhh, I was hoping you could tell me!"

"We need to get help," Henry said, "but first we have to get back to camp. Nobody else knows what's happening, so if Randy, Jackie, or Stu are out of the game, they might be walking into danger just like I did."

"Do you think we can just shout out to them? Warn them?"

"I don't know. I don't think we should give away our position. If all three guys come running after the sound of our voice, we could be in serious trouble."

Erik nodded. "And if I were Randy, Stu, or Jackie and I heard you or me shouting, 'Don't go near the buildings!' I would think it was a trick. It'd make me more likely to run back."

"Right. We just need to get close enough to camp that we can see them and warn them but not close enough to be seen by the killers."

"So when I was dragging you back to camp, I was actually following the plan, even though I didn't know it."

"Yeah, I guess."

"We need to be stealthy."

"Right."

"You're not very stealthy, Henry."

"I know. But I will be. It's like a video game where aliens are attacking the earth, and if you mess up in the game, the aliens come out of your TV screen for real and start disintegrating your family. Because in a real video game, it doesn't matter if you mess up. You just restart or go back to your last saved position. But you have to play *this* video game as well as you can. You can't lose your focus for even a split second because if you do, the aliens will destroy the world. It's like that."

"Or you could just say it's like real life. You don't need all of the video games and alien stuff."

"No, you're not getting what I'm saying. I'm saying that

it's not like a...okay, yes, I didn't need the video game and alien stuff. Thanks, you just screwed up my attempt to inspire myself. Okay, a better way to have phrased this is that we're not playing survival games anymore. This is real, so things that I would have botched during the past week, like stealth, I'm not going to botch now. The stakes are too high. I'm going to rise to the occasion."

If Henry lived through this experience, he was going to write down a more eloquent version of that for the eventual movie version. He wished he had background music, something operatic that switched to electric guitar after his speech was over. Maybe he'd ask Monica about that later.

Anyway, he was now going to become the new Henry that he'd vowed to become a few days ago. The Survival Games were stupid. It was hard to believe that he'd ever even cared about them. Orange paint. Ha! Baby stuff. This was man stuff, and Henry was going to prove that he was the hero that he had recently sort of suspected that he truly could be.

* * *

"What did the man say to the monkey driving a steamroller?" asked Randy.

"I give up," said Stu.

"'Oh, my God, there's a monkey driving that steamroller! That's a definite safety hazard!'"

They walked in silence for a moment.

"Was that supposed to be a joke?" Stu asked.

"Yes."

"Really?"

"The joke is that you thought it was going to have a traditional punch line, but instead the man just said something you'd expect somebody to say if they encountered a monkey driving a steamroller. It subverted your expectations."

"It subverted my expectation that it would be funny."

"Whose car is that?" Randy asked.

"I give up."

"That wasn't a joke setup. There's a real car."

"Oh." Stu shrugged. "No idea. Maybe Max brought in a real chef for our victory dinner."

Randy's stomach grumbled. He always enjoyed a good meal, and by far the worst part of survival camp was that the food was only about fourteen percent edible. When camp ended, the first thing he was going to do was eat an entire sheep, wool and all.

As they walked out of the woods, Randy noticed a man standing near the building. He had a mustache and beard and had kind of an intimidating presence. Probably a friend of Max's.

"Hi!" Randy said.

"Hello there," said the man walking toward them. "How are you?"

"Not too good. I'm dead."

"That so?"

"Yeah." Randy tapped the orange splotches on his shirt. "You know about the Games, right?"

The man shook his head. "No, tell me about the Games."

"You don't know about them? Are you a friend of Max's?"

"Yeah, I'm an old buddy, just checking in. Sorry—I'm Chad."

"I'm Randy. This is Stu."

Stu gave Chad a friendly wave.

"How many people are playing?" asked Chad.

"Now? Just four. I think. Did Henry come back?"

"Henry? Nope, not that I know of."

"Ha!" said Stu, patting Randy on the shoulder. "That means I made the first kill!"

"Well, congratulations," said Chad. "That's quite an accomplishment."

"Thank you."

"Look, I have to be honest with you," said Chad. "I'm here because Max had a family emergency and we're going to take him back into town."

"Oh, jeez, what happened?" asked Randy.

"His sister was in a car accident. So I need to gather all of your fellow campers. Any idea where they could be?"

Randy gestured to the woods. "Anywhere out there. It's against the rules to go past the markers, so they wouldn't be more than a mile away, but I haven't seen anyone else since we started."

"Which sister was it?" Stu asked. "Karen or Jenny?"

"He doesn't have sisters named Karen or Jenny." Chad smiled. "Good try though. You can never be too paranoid."

"Thanks."

"Max was supposed to announce the dead with a megaphone," said Randy, who secretly wished that he'd come up with the idea of asking about imaginary sisters to see if the guy was telling the truth about his reason for being here. "We could use that to call them back."

"That's perfect," said Chad. "Could you do the honors?"

* * *

Jackie flipped back to the first page and began rereading the comic book from the beginning. The X-Men were so cool.

* * *

"Oh, no," Henry whispered as he and Erik very carefully made their way through the woods.

This was unbelievably bad. Randy and Stu were just standing there, having a friendly little chat with one of the psycho killers. (Okay, maybe that was unfair. Henry didn't know for sure that the killers were of the "psycho" variety. In fact, they seemed like fairly sane gentlemen aside from their willingness to take a human life.) It wasn't as bad as, say, finding Randy writhing on the ground with a boa constrictor around his neck, but his best friend was in serious danger.

"You'd better not be lying to me," Erik whispered. "If that's Randy's dad, I will shove this gun down your throat and give you an orange esophagus."

"I'm not lying. He's one of them."

"Should we just shout out? Do you know for sure that he has a gun?"

Henry looked at Chad closely, trying to see if he could detect a gun-shaped bulge under his shirt. "I can't see it, but yeah, I know he does. And there are two other guys. If we call out a warning, they might shoot them."

Erik chewed on his upper lip. "Think we could fake them out with the paint gun?"

"It doesn't look real."

"No, but if we just jumped out there and started screaming and shooting, maybe we could create an environment of confusion or something."

"I think it would be an environment of shredded teenagers."

"Then what? You're the one who knows the enemy. What do we do?"

Henry closed his eyes, hoping that the schematics for an awesome plan would materialize in his brain. What would Max do? What would Indiana Jones do? What would Super Mario do?

Forget that. What would Henry Lambert do?

(He was very pleased to discover that Henry Lambert would *not* say, "*Adios*, suckers! Too bad for you!" and run off screaming into the woods, leaving his friends to their tragic fates. A small part of him had been worried about that.)

"We need to split up," said Henry. "One of us comes out behind the building and distracts them, and during that distraction, one of us gets Randy and Stu to run back into the woods."

"That doesn't sound foolproof."

"It's not. It's so not."

"It's the best we've got without a helicopter or a sorcerer. Do you want to be Team Distraction or Team Shoo Randy and Stu Out of Danger?"

"Which one do you think is more dangerous?"

"Team Shoo."

"I'll take that one. Randy is my best friend."

"You sure?"

"Yeah, we've known each other since kindergarten. Why? Did he say something?"

"No, I meant are you sure you want to do this?"

Henry nodded. "Yes."

"All right. Good luck. Wait for my move." Quickly but with admirable stealth, Erik hurried back through the woods.

Henry watched Randy and Stu carefully. Couldn't they see the murderous glint in Chad's eyes? Couldn't they see that he was a ferocious predator, a barely human monster who would think nothing of murdering socially awkward kids before they'd had their first slobbery tongue kiss?

Erik stepped out of the woods. Henry's insides clenched. He hadn't expected Erik to leave the safety of the trees.

"*Hey, mouth breathers, get your fingers out of your noses, stop your drooling, and come get me! Come on, you sloped forehead simpleton goons! Quit saying, 'DURRRRRR,' and show me what you can do!"*

Chad glanced over, successfully distracted, but in that instant, Henry knew that simply shouting a warning wasn't going to be enough. If there was even a moment of Randy and Stu thinking *Huh? What's going on? Why is Henry shouting at us in this odd manner?* Chad would have time to whip out his gun and blow them away.

Henry had no other choice. He had to attack.

WILDERNESS SURVIVAL TIP!

Stay away from butterflies. They're death machines.

CHAPTER TWENTY-ONE

Items Henry felt would have been useful when he was rushing out to attack a gun-wielding madman: a pitchfork, a pickax, a lightweight lawnmower, a Doberman, a ceiling fan attached to a power source with a cord he wouldn't trip over, ninja stars, an automobile with iron spikes on the front grille, a voodoo doll of Chad, a cow to use as a shield, three machetes tied together, a wheelbarrow filled with broken glass, Jackie Chan, a fully charged Taser, a shockingly vicious gerbil, a water pistol that contained acid instead of water (but not acid that would eat through the gun itself, which would be inconvenient), an aerodynamic wrench for throwing, a backup wrench for bashing, bottle rockets, a chainsaw that would start on the first three tugs, a gun, rotten eggs, Excalibur, a baseball bat (wooden or aluminum—no preference), a shaken-up can of Mountain Dew, one of those metal things you used to poke at burning firewood, an artificial limb (to use as a bludgeoning device, not for locomotion), better shoes, a bullwhip, a bull to whip, some variety of rocket, Captain America's shield, Thor's hammer, Black Widow's costume for Monica to wear, a reliable flamethrower, a spear, an electric razor (which would do no real damage but might cause Chad to stop and think *Why is he running at me with an electric razor?* which could prove to be a deadly lapse of concentration), a potted plant, an orangutan, something with poison on it, a laptop computer that he didn't mind breaking over somebody's head, the power to control space and time, a lengthy screwdriver, a totally badass-looking piece of wood covered with razor wire and rusty nails, roller skates, a tire iron, a javelin—come to think of it, the roller skates wouldn't be very helpful on this uneven dirt ground, so he cancelled that wish—a Model 1881 Gatling gun with the Bruce-style feed system (U.S. Patents 247,158 and 343,532), a pocketknife, a shark, and/or a scimitar.

Sadly, he had none of these things. The only thing close to a weapon that he had access to was a branch and he remembered how well *that* had worked out in the past.

So when he rushed out of the woods, he had no weapons or protection of any sort, except his fingers, which were curled up in a way that he hoped might resemble bear claws but which he knew didn't resemble them all that much.

A very small portion of his brain was occupied with the notion of "Oh, crap, we could be dead three seconds from now!" That portion of the brain was making a checklist of regrets and deciding if he wanted a somber eulogy or an amusing one and wondering if his parents would eventually demand their money back from Strongwoods Survival Camp or if they'd just let it go because it seemed tacky to stop grieving long enough to demand a refund.

A slightly larger portion of his brain believed that he would live much longer than three seconds but that his last minutes of life would be spent lying on the ground, filled with bullets, choking on his own blood. That part of his brain was a total jerk. Not that you could deny the practical nature of what it was saying, but still, Henry didn't want to hear from a whiner right now.

The rest of his brain was operating on pure instinct.

"Run! Run! Run! Run! Run! Run!" he screamed at the top of his lungs as he rushed toward Chad. He hoped that Randy and Stu would realize that he meant for *them* to run and not Chad.

He bashed into Chad with a force that didn't quite match that of a professional football player. In fact, it felt like much of the upper half of his body shattered.

Henry didn't care. Though he would have preferred an outcome where Chad immediately fell to the ground with a great big "*Ooooommmmmphh!*" Henry was cool with what did happen. Chad wobbled for a moment, lost his balance, and fell to the ground with Henry on top of him.

"Run!" he screamed again. He tried to punch Chad in the face; however, Chad was shouting something unintelligible at him and Henry's fist half-went into his open mouth. It was an awkward, off-balance punch and didn't seem to hurt the thug at all.

"Run! Run!" he continued screaming because he was terrified that Randy or Stu would try to help him subdue Chad. Though he wouldn't mind having some assistance, if they didn't get back into the cover of the woods, they were going to get shot by Mr. Grand and Ethan, which would invalidate his own rescue effort.

Randy and Stu ran.

In a truly fantastic world, Henry would grab Chad's gun. He'd love to have Chad's gun now. But in the real world, Henry knew that he was about a sixth of a second from having Chad punch him in the face—a punch that would be significantly more effective than Henry's had been—so he needed to join his friends in their fleeing.

He got up and realized that Chad had foolishly left himself open to the worst kind of kick a human male could receive. The kind of kick that would turn even the mightiest of men into a squealing, whimpering infant. There was no honor in this kick, but these were not honorable times.

Henry kicked him right in the fork in the road.

Chad howled. The sound he made would haunt Henry until the end of his days. Ancient man hearing that noise would have spoken in hushed voices of a creature who had suffered unspeakable tragedy, whose spirit would forever roam these lands. Songs would be written and passed from generation to generation.

Chad clutched at his groin with both hands and emitted a stream of profanity so vile that every baby animal within earshot would be forever corrupted.

Finish him! Henry thought. One more kick and Chad would be no threat to anybody ever again. He'd live out his life in a wheelchair, endlessly weeping, hair permanently white.

But...no. That was a good way to get shot. Instead, Henry ran.

Just as he reached the woods, a gunshot rang out.

He didn't fall to the ground with a bullet hole in his leg, so that was good.

Another gunshot. And another. Henry sprinted, with Randy and Stu running ahead of him, and as long as he didn't do anything ridiculously stupid, Henry thought he was going to escape.

He ran for five seconds without doing anything ridiculously stupid.

And then ten seconds. Still nothing ridiculously stupid. More gunshots.

He wanted to stop and shout, "Ha! Too bad you losers don't have bullets that can weave around trees!" but that would have been ridiculously stupid.

They kept running.

After they ran for thirty seconds, Henry began to believe that he wasn't going to screw this up. He had saved his friends and helped ensure that Chad would not produce more criminal spawn.

Wow. He was a hero.

Then, of course, because he was Henry, he tripped.

But all things considered, it wasn't all that bad of a fall. Randy and Stu glanced back at the sound of Henry hitting the ground with an undignified thud and then hurried back to help him up.

"You okay?" asked Randy.

"Yeah," said Henry. He'd crushed a centipede with his elbow, but he'd mourn its passing later.

All three of them looked back. It didn't seem as if they were being chased.

"That guy wasn't really there to deliver news about Max's sister, was he?" asked Stu.

Henry shook his head. "It's three of them. They killed Max."

"What?"

"I'm serious! Max is dead! They shot him!"

"Max can be punctured by bullets?" Stu asked.

"This isn't something to joke about."

"That wasn't me joking. That was me being stunned."

"So you saved our lives," said Randy.

"That's not important right now," said Henry, even though, yeah, it was important and he hoped they'd seen it all and were prepared to share the story with others. "We just need to find Jackie and get out of here."

It would be a long, miserable walk, but if the five of them were safe, they could eventually find their way back to civilization. Or at least survive long enough to send up a signal to the helicopters that would eventually be searching for them. Henry now believed not only that they could survive but that they wouldn't accidentally blow up the helicopter when it circled. That was the old Henry. The new Henry was awesome.

"Any idea where Jackie is?" asked Henry.

"No, did anybody see which way he ran?"

Randy and Stu said that they hadn't. Henry cursed. With their luck, Jackie could be wandering toward camp right now.

* * *

Jackie sat in the tree, wishing that they'd quit shooting so many blanks. It was distracting him from his reading. He adjusted his position to make himself more comfortable and then started reading the comic book again, wishing he had a digital edition.

* * *

"I think we should shout for him," said Henry.

"Won't that give away our position?"

"It might be worth the risk. We can't just let Jackie go back there."

"Shhhh!" Randy said. "Did you hear that?"

Everybody silently listened.

"What did you hear?"

"Shhhh!"

Off in the distance, a bird chirped a song.

"Is that your bird?" Stu asked.

"No, I don't think it's a bird at all. Doesn't that kind of sound like somebody imitating a bird?"

They listened some more. It did indeed sound like an imitation of a birdsong.

"Is that Jackie?" Stu asked.

"Why would Jackie be doing birdcalls?"

"I don't know. I don't understand the inner workings of Jackie's mind. Maybe he thinks he's a bird."

"Why would he think he's a bird?"

"I just got through saying that I don't understand how that weirdo thinks! I didn't say, 'Oh, that must be Jackie, because it makes perfect sense that he'd be making bird sounds!' All I'm saying is that if we don't think it's a real bird, there aren't that many other options besides Jackie."

"That's fair," said Randy.

The birdsong repeated.

"Make a birdsong back," Randy told Stu.

Stu thought for a moment and then let out a loud...something.

"Not like a chicken! Do it like the one we're hearing!"

Stu chirped out another birdsong.

"You're still doing a chicken!"

"So you do it!"

"Guys, stop it!" said Henry. "Do you really want to get killed because you were arguing about chicken noises?"

"Yeah, knock it off for cluck's sake," said Randy. He looked down at the ground. "I'm sorry. That was very inappropriate. We just needed something to relieve the tension."

"Come on," said Henry, "let's head for the sound. If we get us four together, we can get back with Erik and then find help."

"Do you think Erik got away okay?" Randy asked.

Henry nodded. "Sure. It's Erik. If none of the three of us have been captured or killed, then he sure hasn't."

"Maybe Erik's the one making the bird sounds," said Stu.

"Stop talking, Stu."

It *did* make Henry nervous not knowing for sure that Erik got away, but he was going to remain optimistic. Erik was fine. Totally fine.

The bird sang again. Henry did his own version of a birdsong, which sounded more like a parrot squawking but at least didn't sound like a chicken.

The bird responded.

The bird sounded female.

The bird sounded—and really, there was no reason for Henry to get this out of the birdsong, but he did anyway—like it might be a really attractive girl with black hair.

"I think that's Monica!" he whispered.

"Really?" Randy asked. "How can you tell? Was she making bird sounds to you that you didn't tell me about? I thought we were friends."

"Who's Monica?" Stu asked.

"She was with the girls when they came over, when Max shot up the barracks."

"Why would she ever come back?"

"I don't know. But she had a cell phone last time!"

"That's great!" said Randy.

"If she's coming back after Max shot the place up, she could be deranged," said Stu. "She could be more dangerous than the killers."

"Seriously, Stu, stop talking." The bird sounds weren't coming from that far away, and if they could get in a call to 911, all they'd have to do is find a good hiding place and wait for help to arrive.

They moved through the woods for about five minutes, exchanging birdcalls every minute or so. Henry was going to feel silly if this wasn't Monica or if it turned out to be an actual bird.

Or maybe a cannibal luring them to their doom. That wouldn't be cool. Henry could imagine some filthy, hairy, feral human running its tongue over teeth it had sharpened to points with an emery board, pet rats named Bitey and Gnawy living in its hair, waiting next to a great big metal pot filled with boiling broth and sliced carrots, seasoned with salt and just a pinch of ground-up, dried pancreas. The other cannibals were giggling. "Heh heh heh, you have to be pretty foolish to follow a fake birdcall to a place where cannibals are waiting to dine on you!" And Henry would have to agree. He'd certainly feel sheepish as he shrieked in unbearable agony as they devoured him.

But it probably wasn't cannibals. It was probably Monica.

As it turned out, Henry was absolutely—

WILDERNESS SURVIVAL TIP!
The green part of the tree goes on top.

CHAPTER TWENTY-TWO

"How do you think Henry is doing at survival camp?" asked Henry's mother, dropping some sliced carrots into the stew she was preparing for dinner.

"I think he's doing pretty well," said Henry's father, who had spent the last fifteen minutes trying to think of something clever to tweet. It was a lot of pressure. He didn't want his eleven followers to think he didn't care about his messages.

"Do you think he's getting enough to eat?"

"Yeah, I think they're probably feeding him pretty well."

"Do you think he's getting enough rest? He needs his rest."

"I suppose he's getting enough rest. I don't know. He stays up all night playing those video games, so he doesn't need all that much rest. He's doing fine."

"Do you think he's making friends?"

Henry's father shrugged. "I guess so. Not lifelong friends like he'd make in the army, but he's probably getting along with the other boys there, I assume."

Henry's mother walked over to him with a spoonful of stew. "Here, try this."

Henry's father slurped down the spoonful. "It's good."

"Does it need salt?"

"No, I think it's fine."

"Are you sure?"

"Yes."

"I think it needs salt."

"Then you can add salt. That's not a problem. It wouldn't be bad if it was a little bit saltier, but if it's not saltier, then it's fine too."

"I'm going to add the salt."

"That's fine."

Henry's mom added a few shakes of salt.

"Not *that* much," said Henry's dad. "I thought you were going to add a couple of shakes."

"Oh, sorry. No, I thought it needed more salt than that."

"That's okay. I'm sure it's still fine."

Henry's mom stirred the stew. "Have you heard from Tom and Nancy lately?"

"Not really. I saw Tom when he was walking his dog a couple of nights ago. Maybe it was three nights."

"Did he say anything?"

"Just hi. Why? Is something wrong?"

"Oh, no, no. Nancy had said that we should get together some evening and we never really finalized any plans, so I was wondering if Tom had said something—that's all."

"He didn't say anything about it."

"Okay."

"If it's all the same to you, I'd rather not have us take the initiative on this. If they invite us and we can't get out of it, that's fine, but there's no reason for us to make the push for it to happen."

"Don't you like Tom and Nancy?"

Henry's dad shrugged. "They're okay. Nothing special about them. I don't like the way Tom dribbles when he drinks. He thinks you don't notice, but there's always that one little dribble down his chin."

"Are you sure it wasn't the glass?"

"It might have been the glass once. But I've seen the man drink from at least three different glasses, and there's always a dribble. No, four, because he was at the Barkers' cookout, and this little line of Diet Coke went all the way down his neck."

"What if it's a medical condition?"

"Well, if it's a medical condition, then I apologize for holding that against him. But I don't think it is. I think the man just never mastered the art of beverage drinking."

"Do you want me to ask Nancy about it?"

"No! Are you kidding me? Whether it's a medical condition or not, that's a lose-lose conversation. Don't ask her."

"I won't."

"Good."

"I think I put too much salt in the stew."

"I'm sure it's fine."

"No, I wish you'd stopped me. It's too salty. It's not ruined, but it's not as good as it would have been. I'm sorry."

"Eh, no big deal."

"I know, but I feel bad. At least we're not having company over. Then I'd be really disappointed."

"It's really no big deal. It's just stew."

"You didn't want stew?"

"No, I like stew. I'm just saying that it's no big deal."

"We didn't have to have stew. When I asked if you wanted stew for dinner, you said that sounded fine, but I could have made something else."

"That's not what I'm saying at all. I'm just saying that if it's oversalted, it's not a big deal because it's just stew and not something special." Henry's father quickly realized that this was not the wisest comment he'd made that evening and tried to figure out how to backpedal in the most efficient and safest manner. "Not that your stew isn't special," he said, hoping it would smooth things over but strongly suspecting that it would not.

"Okay," Henry's mother said, by which she meant, "Not okay."

"I think we should invite Tom and Nancy over for lunch tomorrow," said Henry's father. "Maybe even brunch. I really feel bad about judging him for something that might not be his fault and they're good people. What do you say?"

"Whatever you want," Henry's mother said, by which she meant "The stew situation is not resolved."

"Mmmmmm, stew," said Henry's father. "Nothing better than a nice bowl of special stew." This was a truly desperate effort and he knew it. And he knew that she knew it. But this ship was sinking fast and he needed to grab for the nearest life preserver.

Henry's mother said nothing, which was far worse than "Okay" and "Whatever you want."

Henry's father sighed, wishing he were a teenager at survival camp.

* * *

—right.

"Monica!" Henry said, rushing over to her and giving her a great big hug. She clearly hadn't expected him to do such a thing, but she didn't pull away in revulsion.

"Hi," she said after he broke the hug. "I swear I'm not here to mess with your survival games. But I heard the gunshots and it sounded like you guys were having way more fun than

I was, so I snuck out to see how it was going. Are you three in an alliance?"

"No," said Henry. "I'm already dead."

"Me too," said Randy.

"Do you have your cell phone?" asked Henry.

"Yeah."

"I need it!"

"Game withdrawal again?"

"I don't have time to explain," said Henry. "Actually, I do have time to explain because then you'll give me the cell phone quicker. There are three men. I don't know who they are, but they killed our counselor. Shot him dead. I know you think I'm just saying this because I'm too into the Survival Games and I'm having trouble separating fantasy from reality, but I'm not. They were going to kill me. I barely got away."

"He saved us," said Randy.

"We weren't kidnapped or anything," Stu explained, "but apparently, we could have been if Henry hadn't acted."

"He tackled a guy with a gun," said Randy.

"The guy didn't have the gun out when Henry tackled him, but he might have been able to get to it. I didn't see exactly what happened," said Stu.

"Only one of you talk," said Monica. She pointed at Henry. "You talk."

"Anyway, there are three killers out here and they don't want us to rat them out to the police, so they're trying to kill us too. And we're pretty sure our friend Erik got away, but we don't know that for sure. So if you'd let me borrow your phone, I wouldn't use it for gaming, I'd use it to call 911."

Monica handed him the phone. "I would've been okay with

just 'people are trying to kill us.' You're too sweaty for somebody who's not in real danger."

"Thanks." Henry tapped 911 onto the phone display and then held it to his ear.

"What are you going to tell them?" asked Stu. "Should we get our story straight?"

"Why would we have to get our story straight if we're telling the truth?"

"Oh, sorry. I wasn't thinking. It's usually different circumstances when I call the police."

Henry listened for a moment, but the phone didn't seem to be ringing. He glanced at the display. No bars.

"You're not getting a signal," he said, shaking the phone as if that would help. "Why aren't you getting a signal?"

"We're in the middle of the woods."

"But you had a signal last time. You got a text from your boyfriend. I mean, not from your boyfriend, but it was about your boyfriend. Not that I was looking at your texts. We have more important things to discuss right now. A man is dead."

"Don't worry," said Monica. "You're not going to get perfect coverage out here. All we have to do is walk until we get a signal again. No big deal."

They began to walk. Monica didn't acknowledge his comment about her boyfriend. It was possible she agreed that escaping mortal danger took a higher priority than reassuring Henry that he had misunderstood the text and that she had no man in her life and in fact was actively seeking one, somebody skinny who nevertheless could save his friends from ghastly fates, but of course, that wasn't important right now. Escape danger first. Love life second.

"Still no bars," said Henry.

"It's been ten seconds."

"Is there a setting I need to mess with?"

"The phone is on, Henry. You're no good to anybody if you panic."

"I'm not panicking. I'm really not," said Henry, panicking a little. He wasn't sure why. Before Monica showed up, their plan had been to stumble around the woods until they stumbled upon a sign of civilization, so they were much better off now, even if her cell phone signal wasn't immediately working.

"Hello," said a voice, amplified by a megaphone.

It was not the last person Henry wanted to hear saying "Hello," (that would be Satan), but it was the last person Henry wanted to hear from who could realistically be saying "Hello" through a megaphone at that moment.

"We've got your friend Erik," said Mr. Grand. "Show yourself in the next ten minutes or he's dead."

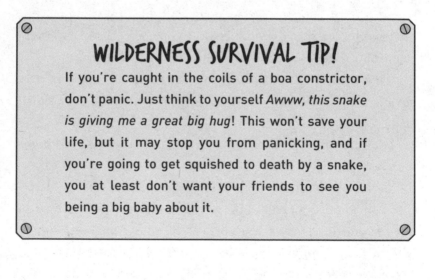

WILDERNESS SURVIVAL TIP!

If you're caught in the coils of a boa constrictor, don't panic. Just think to yourself *Awww, this snake is giving me a great big hug*! This won't save your life, but it may stop you from panicking, and if you're going to get squished to death by a snake, you at least don't want your friends to see you being a big baby about it.

CHAPTER TWENTY-THREE

In retrospect, if he'd known then what he knew now, Erik would not have volunteered to create a distraction. Oh, he couldn't argue that they'd achieved their goal. (Randy and Stu were not currently dead as far as he knew.) But now he was standing outside with a gun about six inches from his face. From his perspective, this hadn't been a good trade-off.

Mr. Grand held the megaphone in front of Erik's mouth. "Tell them," he said. Erik wanted to make a sarcastic comment about germs on the mouthpiece but decided that this wasn't the best time to give the man attitude.

"They've got me," said Erik. There was a momentary instinct to shout "Leave me! Save yourselves!" However, all things considered, he would prefer that his friends actually return to rescue him. So he left that part out.

"You have ten minutes…starting now," Mr. Grand said into the megaphone. "At ten minutes and one second, your friend takes a bullet in the back of the head. Don't be late."

He lowered the megaphone. Chad kept the gun pointed at Erik's head.

"Are you really going to kill me?" Erik asked.

"If we have to," said Mr. Grand.

"Because diplomacy, that's pretty sweet too."

"That's what I've heard."

"Look, I don't know what kinds of things you guys do on a regular basis, but murdering a bunch of teenagers seems really extreme. That's Freddy or Jason stuff. My feeling is that it's not a good solution to your problem."

"Is that so?"

"Yeah, I didn't even witness your crimes. I honestly don't know what you guys did here."

The door opened and Ethan walked out, dragging Max's dead body.

"Sure, don't help me or anything," Ethan muttered, leaving a trail of blood in the dirt as he dragged the corpse to the car.

"I didn't see any of that," said Erik.

"Where some people see challenges, I see opportunity," said Mr. Grand. "There aren't many times in your daily life where you have a legitimate reason to kill teenagers, and you can't just go killing them for no reason. That would be absurd. So this is like a little gift from the heavens."

Erik looked Mr. Grand in the eyes, trying to figure out if he was a deranged whack-job or if he was just pretending to be a deranged whack-job to scare him.

He decided that it didn't matter.

* * *

"What do we do?" asked Randy.

Henry handed the cell phone back to Monica. "I need you to head back to your camp. Call the cops as soon as you get a signal. We're going back."

"We are?" asked Stu.

Monica shook her head. "If these guys are that dangerous, then you'll need me."

"What are you going to do? Take them out one by one?"

"Maybe."

It frightened Henry a little that he totally believed her. "It's more important to call the cops."

Monica gave the phone to Stu. She pointed back the way she came. "Music camp is directly that way. Keep going straight for about three miles. If you don't get a signal by the time you get there, they've got a landline."

"I can't let you do this," said Henry.

"No, she looks pretty strong," Stu noted. "She's a definite asset. Three miles that way. Got it."

"What happens when we show up and we're missing a person? They might kill Erik."

"Was your plan just to hand yourselves over?" asked Monica. "That's a terrible plan."

"Sucky plan," said Stu.

"I wasn't going to just—I don't know what we're going to do yet. But we can't leave Erik there."

"Hey, I like Erik," said Stu. "Nice guy. Good attitude about things. Best hair of any of us except Jackie. But we shouldn't all die for him. He wouldn't die for all of us."

"If he dies, he'll have died for you and Randy."

"Okay, true, but that's not *all* of us."

"No, he'd die for only two of us. That's even nobler."

Stu considered that. "Yes, I'll concede that, but he thought he was going to get away. So he wasn't sacrificing himself for us. He was just putting himself in danger for us, which is still admirable. I'm certainly not trying to take that away from him, but what we're doing is suicide, which is worse than putting yourself in danger. But I do like that idea of walking to music camp."

"It's not suicide," said Henry. "I'm not saying that we should just walk out there and say, 'Here are our heads. Shoot 'em.' But do you really think we should leave Erik without trying to talk to them?"

"I've made my admiration for Erik very clear. If you think that not going back there is the same as leaving him to die, then that's your own issue."

"It's not my issue! That's exactly what it is! Not going back equals dead Erik. Do you want that on your conscience?"

"I have gifts to give to the world and that requires me to be alive. Are you okay with stealing the world's gifts?"

"You're a coward."

"Gift stealer!"

"Stop it!" said Monica. "There's nothing wrong with Stu's cowardice as long as he's serving the greater good."

"Yeah!"

"Now I'm not trying to be insulting about you or egotistical about myself, but you guys need me. Big time. Not trying to toot my own horn here. I just think that I'm the only thing that stands between you guys and this camp being renamed Strongwoods Massacre Camp."

Everybody murmured in agreement. It was sad but true.

"Stu, go find the camp. Don't read any of my texts."

Stu nodded and hurriedly ran off before any further guilt trips could be placed upon him.

"As for the rest of you," said Monica in a tone of voice suggesting that if a movie camera were present, it would be doing a slow, dramatic zoom on her face, "let's go save your friend."

* * *

Jackie grinned as he sat in the tree. He couldn't believe they thought they could draw him out with a fake voice over the megaphone. He was finally starting to get bored with the comic book, so he decided to take a nap.

* * *

Henry and Randy found what they hoped was a safe spot. They were close enough to see the side of the building but had enough tree coverage that the bad guys couldn't get an accurate shot. Hopefully.

"You now have sixty seconds," Mr. Grand said into the megaphone from the front of the building. "Fifty-nine…fifty-eight—"

"We're here!" Henry called out.

"Fifty-seven…fifty-six—"

Mr. Grand couldn't hear them over his own voice. This had the potential of creating a wacky, bloodstained mishap.

"We're here!" Henry and Randy shouted together.

"Good," said Mr. Grand. "Very good."

He walked into view alongside the building only about thirty feet away. Erik followed, hands in the air. Chad had a gun to Erik's back.

"I know that you have no way of calling for help," said Mr. Grand, no longer using the megaphone. "The only weapons you have are toys. Your best bet to survive this is to give yourselves up and let us all talk this out like adults."

"That doesn't really work for us," Henry called out, using his most *Eh, I'm not all that worried that you're gonna kill me* tone of voice. "What else have you got?"

"How about this? Come out or we shoot your friend."

"You're bluffing," said Henry. "You know that if you kill him, you'll never see us again. So make a better offer."

Mr. Grand chuckled. "You're very clever."

"That wasn't clever at all. Don't patronize me."

"We seem to have ourselves an impasse."

"Looks like it."

"How do you propose we resolve it?"

"Let Erik go."

"Why would I do that?"

"You might spend less time in jail."

"Was that a joke?" asked Mr. Grand. "Do you really think that *you're* intimidating *me* in this situation with threats of jail time?"

"Dunno."

"Let me explain how this is actually going to work. Come out now, all of you, or we're going to break your friend. Do you know what a bone sounds like when it snaps in half?"

"Like a snap?" Henry asked.

"So this is all a big joke now? Are you all going to sit out there and giggle while we rip his arms out of their sockets? How about I move things forward for us? Come out now or we're going to shoot a hole through his right palm."

Henry took a deep breath. This was the part of the plan that truly bit.

A really great plan at this point would be based on the following theory:

a) Mr. Grand would not actually harm Erik because

b) If he did, the other kids would flee.

Unfortunately, Henry was nowhere near confident enough about this theory to test it. If they refused to show themselves at all, Mr. Grant and his cronies would most likely make the assumption that:

a) The boys were never going to come out of the woods and therefore

b) They might as well kill Erik.

This was not a desirable outcome, and in fact, it would possibly lead to:

c) Mr. Grand, Chad, and Ethan, assuming that the other boys were close, would recklessly open fire into the woods, figuring that they'd get at least one more of them.

Based on this analysis, the plan of not doing anything was a poor one. So they had to work with a backup theory:

a) If Henry showed himself, Mr. Grand would not necessarily immediately blow him away.

This was a very risky theory since it assumed that a man who wanted very badly to kill Henry would not take the opportunity to do so. In fact, it assumed that all three men would behave in that manner, including one whom Henry had recently kicked in the crotch and whose mind might not be working correctly yet.

However, playing the odds, Henry felt that his immediate status after stepping out of the woods would *not* be to be dead. So he had to do it to save Erik based on his theory that:

a) Monica could actually do what she said she was going to do.

It was insane to think that she could. And Henry wasn't going to lie to himself. If he didn't have a crush on her, his reaction would've been "Are you *kidding*?" Not that he didn't believe girls could accomplish amazing things, but when one of them assured him that she could sneak into the building, find Max's stash of weaponry, and turn it to their advantage…well, he had to be a bit skeptical.

But it was too late now.

Actually, no, it wasn't. There was still time for a wuss-out. Still time to decide that noble behavior was way overrated. Still time to tell his grandchildren "Yep, I was there on that dark day, and though Grampy Henry beat a quick retreat, that's why he's still got a lap for you to sit on."

Henry gave Randy a look that he hoped was meaningful enough if it turned out to be his last one (a brave face yet with a touch of sorrow) and then stepped out of the woods.

"What a complete dumbass," said Chad, incredulous.

"Shut up," Mr. Grand told him. To Henry, he said, "Where are the others?"

"They're watching."

"Tell them to come out."

"No, you wanted to talk like adults, so let's do it. Here's how we're going to solve our problem: We want to get paid. A hundred grand each. We will keep quiet for forty-eight hours after you get out of here, and if we get our hundred grand, then we'll stay quiet for another thousand a month."

"Each?"

"Yes."

"That price seems a bit steep."

"To conceal a murder?" Henry honestly didn't have any idea what the standard blackmail rates for this kind of thing were.

"Why not a make it simple? A flat payment of a hundred and fifty grand each?"

Henry pretended to think that over. "We can do that."

"Then how would I know you wouldn't turn me in as soon as you got your money?"

"Well…that's why I suggested the ongoing payment plan."

"Hmmmm."

Hmmmm was the last comment for a few moments. Henry hoped that his sheen of perspiration wasn't blinding anybody.

"Now, you understand that if you take the money, this makes you an accessory, right? If you take my cash and turn me in, you'll be in the cell next to me. And then my men will find your family and they will die glacially slow deaths. Do you understand this?"

"I do."

"Hmmmm. You know what, Henry? We may just have a deal," said Mr. Grand in what was one of the most transparent lies Henry had ever heard.

"Awesome," said Henry.

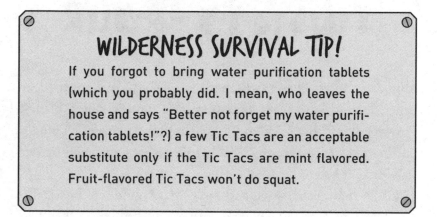

WILDERNESS SURVIVAL TIP!

If you forgot to bring water purification tablets (which you probably did. I mean, who leaves the house and says "Better not forget my water purification tablets!"?) a few Tic Tacs are an acceptable substitute only if the Tic Tacs are mint flavored. Fruit-flavored Tic Tacs won't do squat.

CHAPTER TWENTY-FOUR

Monica's parents liked to say that she was born without the fear gene. She did have fears, but they were more about "What if I'm friendless?" than "What if I get shot by criminals?" Though putting her life in this much jeopardy was extreme even by her standards, it had to be done.

Okay, there were three bad guys. Mr. Grand was busy talking to Henry. Chad was busy pointing a gun at Erik. Ethan had been busy getting rid of the dead body and hopefully would continue being busy with that. So unless there was another bad guy unaccounted for (and Monica thought that Henry had probably counted correctly because three was a pretty low number), all she really had to do was move quickly and hope that Ethan didn't come back inside.

Oh, yeah, and she also had to hope that the back window was unlocked. Henry said that he remembered opening it when they burned a microwavable burrito and it hadn't been locked then, so it most likely wasn't locked now. If it was, she'd have to dive through it, which Monica didn't think you could do without getting a concussion and about seven thousand cuts. If at all possible, she wanted to avoid a plan of action where she got shredded.

She darted out of the woods, moving like the ninja she'd always known she could be. She reached the window, which had approximately eighty-three thousand dead bugs on the sill, and gently but quickly slid it open.

With either the skill of a mighty Olympian or a sneaky burglar, she climbed through the window and then leapt down off the kitchen counter onto the tile floor, landing almost silently.

Nobody was in the kitchen to shoot her. This was a good start.

Though she had no time to waste, she thought it would be a fine idea to take a few seconds to scavenge a weapon or two just in case she had an unexpected visitor. She pulled open the first drawer. A butcher knife. Perfect. You could mess somebody up with a butcher knife.

She opened a cabinet. Plastic glasses. Less useful than the butcher knife. There was also a frying pan, which was not typically stored next to glasses, but whatever. So she grabbed that. It had a thick layer of brownish fossilized-looking gook on the bottom. They actually ate things that had been cooked on this? Vile.

She hurried out of the kitchen, making sure not to step on any of the food (?) that littered the floor. She shifted the frying pan to her left hand, the same one that held the knife, as she went over to the closet door. She turned the handle. Locked.

If she'd had a paper clip and a few extra minutes, she thought, she could pick the lock. But she didn't have either of those, so she hurried across the room toward Max's office.

Oh, jeez, there was still blood on the floor. She stopped, momentarily dizzy. Monica had caused her brothers to have many bloody noses in her life, but actually seeing blood from a murdered human being made her queasy.

Suck it up, girl, she thought. *No, not the blood. Power through this. You don't have time to be sick to your stomach.*

She ignored the blood and rushed into Max's office. A key

ring dangled from a hook next to the door. She grabbed the keys and left the office, thinking that this was going pretty well so far.

She winced. What a stupid thing to think. It was the perfect cue for the door to open.

The door opened.

Her first instinct was to hide, but the only place to hide was under Max's desk. No matter how agile you were, there wasn't much damage you could do to an opponent while crammed underneath a tiny desk. If they made even the most halfhearted effort to search the place, they'd find her, and the best she'd be able to do is let out a girlish little giggle and hope to charm the killers, which was not a fantastic strategy.

So she had to go on the offensive.

She rushed at the door, resisting the urge to let out a primal yell since primal yells tended to alert others in the general vicinity to your presence.

Monica knew that the correct move would be a butcher knife to the throat since the noise would be "*Auuck! Gurgle, gurgle, gurgle!*" instead of the loud "*Clang!*" of a frying pan to the skull. But deep inside, she knew she was not prepared to stab somebody in the neck. It just wasn't part of her personality profile.

She dropped the knife and kept the pan.

As Ethan's eyes widened at the sight of a sixteen-year-old girl charging him (probably not a sight he'd expected at this particular moment), she flipped the pan around and smacked him in the face with the sticky side.

There was a definite *clang*, but it was a muted clang.

Ethan dropped to his knees. The pan stuck to his face.

He clutched at it and tried to pry it off, but the pan remained firmly stuck there. "*It burns!*" he wailed.

Monica kicked the door shut and locked it. She should have

locked it in the first place, but oh well, she'd know that for next time. Then she kicked the pan, which made Ethan thrash around a bit less.

She couldn't see his gun. Maybe he didn't have one. Better to stick with her plan than to waste time searching for a gun that might not be there.

She sprinted for the closet. There were six or seven keys on the ring, none of which were helpfully labeled "This is the key to the closet that has the big black bag full of useful weapons," so she tried the first one, which didn't fit.

Somebody began to pound on the main door. It shook on its hinges. Monica hoped it didn't bring the entire building down.

Ethan stood up, still wailing about how it burned and still trying to tear the pan off his face.

The second key didn't fit.

A gunshot. From…oh, about twenty feet away. So Ethan was packing heat after all. Fortunately, he was still blind and was apparently just shooting in random directions.

The third key fit. Monica opened the closet door just as a bullet put a hole through it. There it was—a big black bag. She picked it up—it was way heavier than she'd expected—and hurried into the kitchen, trying to keep herself from toppling over from the weight of the bag.

Ethan kept pulling the trigger, even though his gun was now just clicking.

She glanced back at him. What if she made Ethan into her hostage? They could do a trade.

No, hostages were more useful when somebody cared about them. Mr. Grand would probably just shrug and say, "He's yours. Use his head as a flowerpot."

Ethan ripped the pan off his face. Monica had never had a wax job, but her understanding was that it was not a pleasant process. Ethan, who'd suddenly had the equivalent of a wax job on his mustache, goatee, and left eyebrow, seemed to agree with that assessment. He bellowed in pain.

The pounding on the front door continued.

Monica ran for the window.

She tossed the bag on the counter, hoping she hadn't just given herself a hernia. As she leapt up there, Ethan let out a primal yell. She could hear his footsteps squeak behind her as she shoved the bag out of the open window.

There was a clatter, a yelp, an even louder squeak, and a thud. Without having seen any of this, Monica thought that he'd probably tripped on the butcher knife and then slipped on the blood and then fell on his butt.

She jumped out of the window. She grabbed the black bag, hurting her shoulder in the process, and then raced into the woods.

* * *

Ethan lay on the floor, not sure if he was looking at his left foot or if his right foot was twisted wrong. He'd tripped on a butcher knife that he hadn't expected to be there, slipped on the blood that he should have known to avoid, and fallen on his butt. He wasn't sure if the pain or the shame was worse.

He was definitely looking at his right foot, so the pain was worse.

The door burst open, the top hinge popping right off. "What happened?" Chad asked.

"What do you *think* happened?" Ethan said, hoping that Chad would not draw the conclusion that he'd been defeated by a teenage girl.

Chad ran over and looked in the closet. "Where is he?"

"I don't know!"

"Is he still here?"

"I don't know!"

"What happened to your facial hair?"

"It was horrible!"

Chad looked into the kitchen and then back at Ethan. "He must've gone out the window! Who was it?"

Ethan wondered if a lie would come back to haunt him. He suspected that it would but decided it was worth the risk. "A great big kid! Giant kid! Maybe not even a kid!"

Chad cursed. "We need to forget about the kids and get out of here."

*　*　*

Randy slammed Monica's pocketknife into the second tire of Mr. Grand's car. He, Henry, and Monica had been worried the men would just leave, taking Erik with them, but this would put a stop to that.

*　*　*

"What's going on in there?" Mr. Grand called out at the sound of a *clang*.

Ethan didn't answer.

Mr. Grand, Chad, Henry, and Erik listened carefully, with Mr. Grand and Chad hoping there wouldn't be any more surprising noises and Henry and Erik hoping there would be all kinds of them.

When the gunshots started, Mr. Grand nodded to Chad. "Check it out."

Chad ran off. Now, instead of each of them having a man point a gun at them, Henry and Erik were being shared by Mr. Grand's gun. Henry didn't feel significantly safer.

* * *

Randy had nearly had a heart attack when Ethan went into the building; however, he'd been on the other side of the car and Ethan didn't see him. Randy slammed the pocketknife into the last two tires, nearly having another heart attack when Chad came running around the corner. Had Chad not been so distracted by pounding on the door, he probably would have at least seen Randy's elbow, but he didn't.

With all of the tires flat, Randy scampered back into the woods.

* * *

As the last gunshot rang out, Henry cried out, clutched at his chest, and fell to the ground.

CHAPTER TWENTY-FOUR AND A HALF

"Hi, everybody, this is Rad Rad Roger, coming to you live from the holding cell at my favorite local police station. They wouldn't let me bring my camera crew or even a camera, but that's okay! Rad Rad Roger is gonna do his show anyway!"

"Hey, shut up!"

"I haven't finished reading *I Have a Bad Feeling About This*, but it looks like our main character, Henry, just died, which is weird because I was talking to him and he didn't say anything about dying. Maybe he did and I don't remember. Rad Rad Roger has had a lot to drink tonight. Is it still tonight?"

"You want to get shanked? Shut up!"

"Anyway, even though he died, it was good to see Henry find his courage and be a hero and stuff. It's too bad he died before he could hook up with Monica. I guess there are still a few more chapters left in the book, so anything could happen, but I think we should shift gears and talk about Sandy Klifton's baby bump!"

"I warned you!"

"Uh-oh, this is Rad Rad Roger, signing off for AAACCCK!!!"

CHAPTER TWENTY-FIVE

Henry's life did not flash before his eyes because he was totally faking it. Though he'd been told quite clearly not to move, he thought that Mr. Grand would make an exception for him getting shot. As he dropped to the ground, Henry hoped that Mr. Grand wouldn't say, "Oh, well, he's been shot anyway. Might as well put a couple more in his head."

He also hoped that Erik would use this opportunity to do... something. Henry wasn't sure what. He didn't care as long as it turned out to be useful.

Erik cried out and dropped to the ground.

Henry didn't see a bullet hole in the side of the building, so he was pretty sure that Erik was faking it too. It wouldn't take long for their scheme to come unraveled. Henry wished he had a packet of ketchup handy to smash against his chest.

"How stupid do you think I am?" asked Mr. Grand. It was clear from his tone that the correct answer was not "Stupid enough to think that both of you just got shot."

Mr. Grand cursed as something hit him in the face.

* * *

Ha, thought Randy, who could tell that Henry and Erik were faking. Nobody could say that he couldn't throw a rock well when the need arose!

* * *

The boys attacked.

Henry went for Mr. Grand's right leg, Erik went for his left leg, and together they pulled him off balance. Mr. Grand's head smacked into the side of the building and he fell to the ground, not moving.

Erik pulled the gun out of his hand.

"Go!" Erik whispered, gesturing for Henry to run back into the woods.

"I'm not leaving you!"

"I'm not staying behind, you geek! Go before they come back! Go! Go! Go!"

Henry and Erik rushed back into the woods. Henry wondered if it was a bad idea not to shoot Mr. Grand while he lay there, knocked out. In a movie, he'd probably be all like "Shoot him, you fools!" but in real life, murdering an unconscious human being seemed wrong, even if that unconscious human being would happily murder you while you were unconscious.

They immediately joined up with Randy and continued running through the woods, barely able to believe that they'd gotten away. Henry already wanted to start talking about how much they rocked, but there'd be time for that later.

"Hold on a second," he said, stopping. He let out a birdcall and they all listened carefully for a response.

Monica let out a birdcall back—a somewhat pained-sounding birdcall but a birdcall nevertheless. She was okay!

"We did it," said Erik.

"Do you think we should have shot him?" asked Henry.

"I don't know about you, but I kind of like that I won't have horrible nightmares about what I've done."

"Yeah, good point." Henry let out another birdcall. Monica responded, closer this time.

Once again, there was no evidence that the men were coming into the woods after them. Henry was almost a little disappointed by this. If Mr. Grand, Ethan, and Chad would chase after them in a blind rage, screaming something ridiculous like "You're doomed! Dooooooomed!" Henry felt that he and the others could take them out.

He also knew that he was probably wrong about this and that it was quite fortunate that the evil men weren't chasing them.

He did another birdcall. Monica responded.

"I'm sure they've figured out those aren't real birds," said Randy. "You could probably just speak in English."

Henry had been thinking the same thing, but the birdcalls felt somewhat more romantic. Not that he was thinking in romantic terms. There was a time and place for such feelings and it wasn't after nearly being…well, no, actually, immediately after surviving almost certain death was the *perfect* time for thoughts of romance. The only way it could've been better is if he'd put his life at risk for her instead of vice versa.

And then, there she was.

She was sitting on the ground next to the big black bag. She'd done it! They didn't really *need* the weapons anymore, but it was awesome that they had them just in case. The bag was open and many of its wonderful contents, like rifles, were spread around.

Monica didn't look quite as happy as Henry would've hoped, but she did give him a big one-armed hug. His initial thought— that she was too repulsed by him to embrace him with both arms, which he supposed was a reasonable repulsion—was eased when she showed him how badly swollen her arm was. Not that he was happy that her arm was injured, but he'd rather have her arm hurt than to have her not like him.

That sounded really selfish. He was glad he hadn't said it out loud.

"I thought you said he kept the ammo in the bag," said Monica.

"He does. He keeps everything in the bag."

Monica shook her head. "There's no ammo in here. Unless we want to go after them with one bow and a few arrows, this stuff is worthless."

"Oh," said Henry. "Well, that's not cool."

"Nope."

"It's fine though," said Randy. "Stu's on his way to get help and none of us are kidnapped anymore, so we can just get out of here."

Monica held up the key ring. "We could go for Max's car, but I guess it's better to just hike to music camp."

"Yeah, we don't want to take another big risk," said Henry. "Maybe we'll catch up to Stu."

* * *

Still no signal. This was ridiculous. They should have *extra* cell phone coverage in the middle of the forest, not less, because this is when people needed it most!

Stu sighed with frustration. At least he was still walking in the right direction. That is, at least he was ninety percent certain he was still walking in the right direction. Or had been a few minutes ago. Now it was closer to a fifty-fifty thing.

He did not have the slightest freaking clue where he was going.

How could the others have been so stupid as to trust him with this task? Walk straight. Yeah, right. Unless you possessed the ability to magically pass through trees, which Stu did not, you couldn't walk straight in the woods. Even without the trees, the ground was all bumpy and it kept sending you off course.

He was going to die, and thus, everybody else was going to die. This wasn't how he wanted to perish. He wanted to perish by being shot out of a cannon when he was ninety-five. Dying of starvation alone in the woods wasn't nearly as cool.

He heard something.

A growl.

Not a human growl.

Not a cheerful growl.

Stu would be extremely pleased if this was not a bear.

It could be anything. Lots of things growled. Harmless, adorable little forest creatures like bushy-tailed squirrels or chubby-cheeked chipmunks. Maybe it was even a baby bird with a vocal defect.

Stu froze as something moved not too far ahead of him.

It was partially hidden by the trees, but it was way bigger than a chipmunk.

It was brown, hairy, and approximately the size of a bear. This didn't necessarily mean that it was a bear. It could have been a squirrel that somehow shared the dimensions of a bear, although that would be even more frightening than a regular bear.

The animal stepped into plain view.

Yep, it was a bear.

Stu tried to remember what you were supposed to do if you encountered a bear. Were you supposed to make lots of noise and rush at it, with the assumption that a bear was more afraid of you than you were of it? Or were you supposed to back away quietly, saying "Nice bear…nice bear—" in a trembling voice?

If he could get a cell phone signal, he'd google it.

He did know that you weren't supposed to run away, unless your goal was for the bear to pounce on you and start devouring your back.

So he'd go for calmness. Calmness was the key.

The bear looked at him.

Stu whimpered.

He wished he had some bear snacks available—that is, besides his own flesh.

"Hello, Baloo," he said, backing away in frame-by-frame slow motion. "How's everything going with you? Having a pleasant afternoon? I trust your hibernation went well this year?"

The bear stepped forward toward him.

Stu's hand suddenly became drenched with about a quart of perspiration and Monica's phone slipped out and fell to the ground.

He crouched down, but the bear's growl grew louder, as if it were suggesting that retrieving the phone was not a good idea. He didn't think the bear actually wanted the phone for itself. The phone was a couple of years out of date and the front was all scratched up—and also, this was a bear—but he decided to leave the phone behind.

He knew he shouldn't run, but as the bear charged at him, he decided to anyway.

✳ ✳ ✳

Mr. Grand's rage was so intense that he wanted to rip off Ethan's other eyebrow. But he restrained himself. This was no time to lose control and you couldn't just rip somebody's eyebrow off with your fingers anyway.

Once this situation was resolved, he had every intention of beating either Ethan or Chad to death. Probably not both of them, but one of them for sure. It would make him feel better. He'd listen to a soothing Beethoven symphony while he did it.

Chad was busy trying to hot-wire Max's truck but having no luck.

"I don't know if this makes you feel any better," said Ethan, "but kids these days, they aren't like when we were kids. They're faster and stronger. They've got more minerals in the water and stuff, so if they get the best of us, it's really not as disgraceful as you might think."

"Do you believe deep in your heart that there was any possibility that comment would make me feel better?"

"Well, no," Ethan admitted. "But it makes me feel better."

"It shouldn't," said Mr. Grand. "What's happened here today is pathetic on a cosmic scale. You were hit in the head by a frying pan. There is nothing redeemable about that."

Ethan shrugged. "At least we killed Max. That's what we came for, right? Mission accomplished."

Mr. Grand wanted to lunge at the eyebrow but regained his composure. "Don't talk," he said. "Don't ever talk again. Live the rest of your life as a mute. Imagine that any time you open your mouth, a giant fist will slam into it because that's exactly what's going to happen!"

Mr. Grand cursed silently. He was so upset by this turn of events that he was making threats that had only a tiny fraction of his usual wit and menace. Imagine that a giant fist will slam into it? How inept.

"How's it going?" he asked Chad.

"Is that rhetorical or do you want the real answer? Because the real answer is crap."

"Give me the crap answer."

"This isn't working. This truck is one step up from a

make-it-yourself pinewood derby car. I honestly don't know how it even runs. I'd have more luck hot-wiring a Martian spacecraft."

"Wonderful. Just wonderful." Mr. Grand wanted to kick something, anything. Preferably something with bones inside. He'd just gotten off the blood pressure medication, but his capillaries were going to explode if they didn't catch some sort of lucky break.

"Hey, what's going on?" asked a small green-haired kid, walking over to the truck.

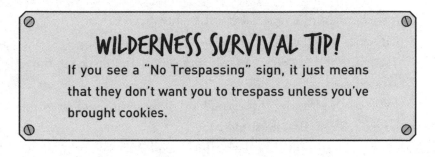

WILDERNESS SURVIVAL TIP!

If you see a "No Trespassing" sign, it just means that they don't want you to trespass unless you've brought cookies.

CHAPTER TWENTY-SIX

"Gentlemen," said Mr. Grand over the megaphone. "It appears that we have another special guest to introduce to you!"

"It's me," said Jackie. "Sorry."

Henry, Randy, Erik, and Monica simultaneously let out a frustrated sigh.

"Well," said Randy, "I for one kind of thought that was going to happen. Wish I'd said something."

"It's the same deal as last time," said Mr. Grand. "Show yourself or he dies. And this time, I promise you that we are not bluffing."

"Does that mean they were bluffing the first time?" Erik asked. "Because I've gotta say, I had that gun to my head and I didn't get the feeling that anybody was bluffing."

"At least we weren't arrogant about what we thought was our victory," Henry said. "That would make this sting a lot worse."

Everybody let out another frustrated sigh.

"Here's what we've got," said Monica. "A few rifles without any ammunition—"

"I've got a gun," Erik told her, holding up the gun he'd taken from Mr. Grand and making everybody flinch a bit. "Thank God for the Second Amendment."

"I'm pretty sure the Second Amendment has nothing to do

with a gun you stole from somebody who was trying to kill you," said Henry.

"Hey, this gun might save your life!"

"I'm not saying it won't come in useful. I'm just saying that it being useful has nothing to do with a constitutional amendment. You swiped it from a gangster. I'm sure it's not a legally registered weapon." Henry wasn't sure why he felt the need to debate this. Had he been possessed by the spirit of Stu? And did this mean Stu was dead?

"These guys aren't actual gangsters," said Erik.

"Sure, they are."

"No, they aren't. A gangster would be somebody who—" Erik trailed off. "Okay, I don't know what specifically defines a gangster. I didn't think it was these guys, but I might be wrong."

"May I continue?" asked Monica, not using her most polite tone of voice.

"Yes, I'm sorry. You know what it was? I was thinking that gangsters wore those pinstripe suits. That was really stupid of me. I'm exhausted and stressed out from the whole gun-in-my-face thing. Ignore me."

Monica did. "We've also got a bow and some arrows."

"That's perfect," said Randy. "Henry's a master archer."

"Good," said Monica, handing Henry the bow.

"I'm kind of overrated," Henry admitted. "Maybe you should take it."

"I've never shot a bow and arrow in my life. I'm only good with bludgeoning weapons."

"Okay, I'll take it. But I want it out in the open that I'm a complete archery fraud. I don't want anybody to think that I put Jackie's life in danger out of my own pride."

"Noted. We also have canteens, sticks—why are there sticks

in here?—matches, water purification tablets…nothing useful in a siege."

"Are there grenades?" Randy asked.

"No."

"Darn. I thought there'd be grenades."

"All right," said Henry, "so this isn't as good as a machine gun or pack of dynamite. That's fine. We're not the same wieners we were when we started Strongwoods Survival Camp and we're not afraid to go on the offensive! We're going to show those scumbags that they can kill the strongest of us but they can't kill the weakest!" Henry considered that for a split second. "That's not at all what I meant to say, and right now I can't think of a better way to phrase it, so be inspired by what I meant instead of what I said!"

The others did not seem intensely motivated.

"We've been the underdogs long enough," said Henry. "Everybody laughs at us. Maybe they don't laugh at Monica so much and maybe not Erik. But Randy and I get laughed at all the time and we're tired of it! That changes now. This is our moment! This is our time of redemption! And like all good times of redemption, there's the chance that we'll mess it up and need even more redemption when we're done, but I'm willing to take that risk! I think we can do this! And in the end, that's what life is all about—carefully calculated risk! *Let's do this!*"

After some more brief discussion, everybody reluctantly decided that yes, they should probably do this. The warriors headed off into battle.

* * *

Jackie had discovered that having a gun pointed at you made you blink a lot. It also made you ask the person to please not point the gun at you, although so far, the man hadn't agreed to stop doing it. It wasn't as scary as being threatened by, say, a buzzing chainsaw, but Jackie's heart was racing. His legs were trembling and he was crying a little bit.

They sat inside the dining hall. Both of the men (a third was outside in Max's truck) seemed really unhappy, especially the one with weird facial hair. Jackie had thought that his own green hair was punk rock, but this guy looked like he'd actually ripped his facial hair right out. His face was even bleeding a little. Now *that* was hardcore.

The other man, the one who was pointing the gun at him, had an extremely red face and kept massaging his forehead with his free hand. It had clearly been a very stressful day for these men.

"You're not going to kill me, are you?" Jackie asked.

"We very well might."

"What did I do?"

"You were in the wrong place at the wrong time, kid."

Jackie nodded. "So it's not anything about me personally?"

"Nope."

"Okay. Good." Jackie didn't want to die, period, but if it did happen, at least it wasn't because these guys didn't like him.

⋇ ⋇ ⋇

Chad yelped as the wires shocked him for the sixth time. But his attitude brightened as the truck roared to life.

"Bring the kid out!" he shouted. "We're good to go!"

Mr. Grand, Ethan, and the green-haired kid hurried outside. They squeezed into the truck and slammed the door shut.

"Where are you taking me?" asked the kid.

"Someplace bad," said Mr. Grand with a grin. "Someplace very, very bad."

Chad put the truck into reverse and they pulled out of the parking spot. Chad wasn't one hundred percent sure which bad place Mr. Grand was talking about; however, he could think of at least three possibilities back at home, and he was glad he wasn't that kid. Real glad.

* * *

At the sound of the engine, Henry, Randy, Erik, and Monica picked up their pace. This couldn't be good. Well, it *could* be good if that was the police who'd mastered the art of teleportation or who just happened to be doing a clarinet bust at the music camp. Or it could be good if Mr. Grand and his associates just said, "You know what? This whole kidnapping thing is quite a bother. Let's leave the youngster here safe and sound and go on our merry way."

But no. Henry could see Max's truck and Jackie was in there with the bad guys.

"I'm gonna try to shoot out the tires," said Erik.

"No, no, no!" said Monica. "They know how many shots you have and they'll know if you run out! They can't know we're out of ammo! Save the bullets! Henry, *you* shoot the tires!"

There was no time for Henry to say, "What? Who? Me? But I already said that I'm not an adept archer! Somebody else should take on this enormous responsibility!" This needed to be the most important arrow he'd shot in his life and the fact that it was only arrow number two did not detract from the enormity of the task at hand.

He grabbed the arrow that Monica held toward him, notched it, took not-so-careful-because-the-truck-was-only-about-fifty-feet-away-and-there-wasn't-time aim, and launched the arrow.

It sailed through the air, straight and true.

Then it continued to sail through the air right over the truck.

"Shoot more of them! Shoot more of them!" said Monica, handing him another arrow. He notched it and shot.

This time, the arrow struck the front hood of the truck, shattering into three pieces on impact. The truck screeched to a halt, but then, the moment of confusion apparently resolved, the tires squealed as the truck rocketed forward, the gas pedal to the floor.

"Shoot more! Shoot more! Shoot more!" said Monica.

"More! More! More!" said Randy, agreeing with her.

Henry notched another arrow. What he lacked in accuracy he would make up with quantity. This arrow struck the windshield, creating a giant spiderweb pattern in the middle of the glass. He knew there was a chance that he was creating a horribly ironic moment ("How sad that Henry slew the kid he was trying to protect! It pretty much sucked every bit of joy out of his accomplishment."), but he had to go for it.

He notched another arrow and tried to imagine that he was Katniss Everdeen from *The Hunger Games*. She wouldn't miss. Katniss wouldn't have any self-doubt. She would launch the arrow at her target, knowing that it would land exactly where she intended.

Or maybe she did have self-doubt. Maybe she had to imagine herself as Robin Hood. That's what Henry would do. He'd imagine that he was Katniss imagining herself as Robin Hood. Or maybe William Tell. No, wait. He couldn't remember if William Tell had successfully shot the apple off his son's head or if it ended sadly.

Whether it was winning a brutal competition in a dystopian society, robbing from the rich to give to the poor, or saving an emotionally needy green-haired kid from gangsters, they were all true heroes. Henry could feel the heroism of those who'd come before, even if they were made-up characters, flowing through his veins. They guided his string-pulling-back hand. They swiveled his eyeball to the exact right place to take perfect aim.

There was total silence. Either Henry had achieved total concentration, or he'd suddenly gone deaf. He hoped it was total concentration.

Henry Lambert released the arrow.

The *swish* sounded like a heavenly choir, albeit a heavenly choir that sang in swishing sounds instead of beautiful voices.

The arrow sailed through the air, slicing through trillions of air molecules…and then it struck the truck's tire.

As with the targets from before, Henry had been aiming for a different tire, but he didn't care. "I did it!" he cried out as the truck screeched to another halt. "Five hundred points!"

Monica gave him a quizzical look.

"Sorry," said Henry. "I almost got through that whole thing without thinking about it in video game terms."

"Shoot again! Shoot again!"

Henry notched another arrow and fired, puncturing the tire he'd been aiming for the first time. He *was* an archery master! He made Katniss and Robin Hood look like bumbling fools who didn't know which way the pointy end should go!

The truck veered off course, smashed into a tree, and stopped moving.

Randy picked up a rifle. "Let's finish them off!" he shouted.

Before anybody could say, "What do you expect to do with a rifle that has no ammo?" Randy showed them what he expected to do with a rifle that had no ammo. He flung the rifle at the truck, hitting and shattering the windshield, and then reached for another as the others joined in.

WILDERNESS SURVIVAL TIP!

If you run out of food on your camping trip, the cheat code is MHYM-213-66198-G.

CHAPTER TWENTY-SEVEN

As the second tire deflated, Mr. Grand screamed for Chad to floor the gas pedal, which he'd been doing since the first arrow. The truck went out of control and smashed into a tree. Well, three trees to be accurate.

"You idiot!" Mr. Grand shouted, as if it were Chad's fault that the forest contained inconveniently placed vegetation.

"At least they don't—" Ethan's sunshiny and optimistic observation, whatever it might have been, was cut off as a rifle struck the windshield, spraying glass bits all over them.

Another rifle hit the front hood.

"What are they doing?" Mr. Grand demanded because the answer of "Flinging weapons at our vehicle" seemed too bizarre to be the correct answer.

A canteen struck the driver's side window, cracking but not shattering the glass.

"I'm getting out of here!" shouted Chad, throwing open the door. He knew Mr. Grand would fire him and then send other associates to kill him and then send other associates to kill his family, but he couldn't just let himself get clobbered to death by weapons thrown by geeky teenagers. That was no way to end what had been a pretty decent career in the criminal arts.

Chad got out of the truck just in time to be bonked on the

head by a canteen. It wasn't filled with water, so it was more embarrassing than painful.

Then a rifle hit him in almost the exact same spot, which was more painful than embarrassing.

Chad clutched at his head and ran. Another canteen got him, this one striking his fingers right where they clutched at the rifle wound, which did not feel good. Another canteen missed his head but landed right where his foot touched the ground in the process of running, causing him to make a noise that was not representative of his standard dignity. He fell, somehow managing to bash his head in the same place.

Instead of lying on the ground and crying until the police showed up, which sounded like a nice plan at the moment, Chad got back up and staggered forward, wishing the world would come back into focus. He stumbled and fell again, which did not make things less blurry, and then got back up and continued staggering, praying that another canteen would not hit him.

Something else smacked him in the head. It was a water purification kit, although Chad was too dizzy to know that. He continued running, looking for sanctuary, anyplace he could be protected from this onslaught. Though he would never, ever admit this to anybody, he wanted his mommy.

There! A building just ahead! Safety! Sweet, sweet safety! He'd barricade himself inside there until he felt his own sanity begin to return!

Chad opened the door to the barracks and slammed it closed behind him, gasping for breath and almost sobbing with relief. They couldn't find him here. Nobody could find him here. He was safe! Safe! Ha! Ha-ha! Ha-ha! Safe! Ha!

Did giggling over stuff that wasn't funny mean you'd gone crazy? He was pretty sure it did. But being locked inside his own giggly mind was better than the situation in the real world, so he was okay with that.

Something chirped.

It sounded like a bird, though in his current mental state it could have also been a rhinoceros.

Chirp. Chirp. Chirp.

He looked around the barracks; however, his vision was still blurry and he couldn't see anything except a little dot that seemed to get bigger and bigger until—

"Aaaaiiiiiiiieeeeee!!!" Chad remarked as the bird began pecking at his face. He ran around, flapping his arms as if he might be able to fly too until he crashed into a cot. He fell to the floor and hit his increasingly fragile head once again. This time, his brain said, "Okay, I've had enough of this" and shut down into unconsciousness.

This was nice for Chad because otherwise he would have felt it as Randy's bird pecked, pecked, pecked at his head. The bird had had plenty of rest over the last few days and didn't get tired of doing this anytime soon.

* * *

"He left us!" Ethan wailed. "He left us!"

"We don't need him," said Mr. Grand as about a dozen small rocks hit the truck at once.

Jackie didn't think that Mr. Grand and Ethan would just let him excuse himself and leave the truck, but he felt that this was probably a pretty good opportunity for him to take advantage of the chaos. So he grabbed Mr. Grand's nose between his index finger and thumb and gave it a great big twist.

Mr. Grand howled in pain.

Jackie began punching Mr. Grand in the stomach over and over again. Then a rock hit him on the shoulder and he realized that his friends were not necessarily the most accurate projectile hurlers in the world. An arrow sailed past his face and he yelped.

⁂

Henry lowered the bow. He'd gotten overconfident about his arrow-shooting abilities and almost skewered Jackie. That wasn't cool. He needed to remember that he was still basically incompetent and plan his moves accordingly.

As far as Henry knew, there was a gun remaining in play, but Ethan didn't seem to be taking advantage of that. "I'm going in," said Erik, holding up the gun he'd stolen from Mr. Grand and then rushing out onto the road.

"Freeze!" Erik shouted, sounding like he practiced it in the mirror every morning. "Let Jackie go!"

Ethan did not freeze. He opened the passenger-side door and then fled, speed-limping back toward the buildings. Clearly, he felt that Erik would not shoot him in the back.

Henry hoped Erik wouldn't shoot him in the back. That would end things on kind of a downer note.

"I'm going after him," said Randy.

"What?" Henry asked. "Why?"

"Because he's a loose end. If we let him run away, the tables could turn again, and somebody else could get kidnapped. It could be you or me getting kidnapped next, and I won't allow that to happen!"

"Don't you think we're more likely to get kidnapped if we go after him instead of just letting him run away?"

Randy considered that. "C'mon, Henry, everybody else got their big moment."

"Two of them ran away. Were you going to go after both of them?"

"No. Just one. I mean, I'm not dumb."

"He's right," said Monica.

"Who? Me or him? About which part?" asked Henry.

"Can I finish?"

"Yes."

"Randy's right."

"About not being dumb?" asked Randy.

"We need to take them out now. Henry, you keep Erik covered while he keeps Mr. Grand covered. Randy and I will go after the other two guys."

Henry didn't like the idea of them splitting up, but they had a point. It was best to finish off Ethan and Chad while they were at their most laughably pathetic. "All right," he said, "but promise me that Monica will go after whichever one is harder to beat."

"I promise," said Monica. Then she gave him a kiss on the cheek and she and Randy hurried off.

Henry just stood there, stunned. She'd kissed him. The location and duration of the kiss weren't anything more than he'd expect from his grandmother, but still...she'd kissed him. She didn't consider him a repulsive troglodyte. Even if it wasn't a "*muah-muah-muah-muah*[slobber][slobber]" kiss, he could now say that he had been kissed by Monica.

He could die now, happy.

Though he preferred not to die now. And in fact, it was probably best for his continued survival if he stopped thinking about the peck on the cheek (he hoped there was a lipstick stain there as proof, though Monica didn't look like she was wearing lipstick) and focus on the extremely dangerous events unfolding in front of him.

Mr. Grand got out of the truck, holding Jackie in front of him by the hair.

"Let him go!" said Erik.

"Put the gun down or I'll break his neck," said Mr. Grand.

"I'm serious! Let him go or I'll shoot!"

"You think I can't snap this little twerp's neck like a tooth-pick?" Mr. Grand asked. "Drop the gun. Now."

Henry notched the last of his arrows. Jackie was pretty short, so both he and Erik had a reasonably clear shot at Mr. Grand, but neither of them were professional marksmen. What if he took the shot and hit Jackie instead? When people wrote about their amazing victory, the stories would contain an asterisk, like the world records held by disgraced athletes who used performance-enhancing drugs.

(*Henry shot his friend in the face with an arrow by mistake, so it's important to note that when you take all of the elements into consideration, he's not all that awesome. In fact, Jackie's parents think he pretty much sucks.)

(**Also, while Henry and Erik were all like "Oh, no! Jackie is dead!" Mr. Grand escaped and he was so mad that he went on a killing spree, all of which we can safely blame on Henry as well. One of the people who died would have become a legendary pediatrician, saving the lives of hundreds of children. Henry, if you're reading this footnote, you're a total douche.)

(***Henry is not reading this footnote, though, because an angry mob stormed his house and carried him away. Serves him right.)

Henry couldn't tell if Erik was going to lower the gun or not. Mr. Grand twisted his handful of Jackie's hair, making him wince.

"Now, Erik! Do you want his death on your conscience?"

Erik did not look like he was going to lower the gun. Erik was closer to the villain, but from Henry's angle, a much larger section of Mr. Grand was exposed. Henry needed to take the shot.

He envisioned a tiny little target on Mr. Grand's side, with an arrow above it pointing down and a flashing sign saying "Shoot here."

He shot the arrow.

It took about a thousandth of a second for Henry to realize that this arrow was not going to hit the target. Erik cried out and dropped the gun as the arrow went right through his arm.

Henry gasped. That was not *at all* what he'd meant to do. And since he was the only one with a bow, it was going to be difficult to pretend that he didn't do it.

Erik dropped to his knees, screaming in pain.

Mr. Grand shoved Jackie aside and went for the gun.

Henry rushed out of the forest.

* * *

Though he'd never admitted it to any of his coworkers, this was not the first time Ethan had been defeated by scrawny teenagers. It wasn't even the second time. If he survived this, Ethan vowed that he would never again go near anybody between the ages of thirteen and eighteen. They brought nothing but misery to his life.

He limped toward the buildings, trying not to think about how much his face hurt. Facial hair was not supposed to be ripped out like that.

Not that he could tell anybody how much his face hurt or they'd say "Your face hurts? Well, it's killing me too!" He knew they would. And then they'd laugh and laugh, as if they'd made that joke up themselves.

The buildings were too obvious of a place to hide—nobody would be stupid enough to choose them—so he hurried past them, figuring that he would just limp through the woods until he found civilization or until he ran off the edge of a cliff and fell to his death.

No, wait—an outhouse!

Nobody would look for him in an outhouse.

He opened the door, went inside, and then quickly shut the door behind him. The aroma was not the finest he'd ever inhaled, but it wasn't the worst either. And as long as nobody needed to actually use the facilities, he could wait here until things calmed down.

But what if somebody *did* need to use the outhouse? What if it was that violent girl? Ethan didn't think he could handle another beating.

He lifted the lid and gazed down into the darkness below. He now had a very important decision to make. What he chose to do next could save his life, but it could also haunt him until the end of his days.

He didn't want to go to jail. Could two or three days down there be worse than spending the rest of his life in prison? He could always get therapy.

He said a silent prayer and then lowered his right foot into the hole.

What was that?

Had that sound come from below?

Ethan froze, listening carefully.

Was something *slithering* down there?

Ethan continued to listen. He thought he heard a soft rumble, like some unearthly beast was rising from an ancient slumber. What sort of nightmarish creature lurked beneath his feet? If he'd proceeded with his original plan, he would have been devoured! Or was it possible that this outhouse was the portal to the very pits of hell?

"No...*no*—" he whispered. He'd never felt such fear, such terror. This outhouse was a place of great evil, a structure into which nobody should ever venture, and the only way to save humanity was to burn it to the ground!

He realized that tears were streaming down his cheeks, but he didn't care. There was no shame in weeping in the presence of something this scary. He was standing near things that no human being should ever stand near.

The slithering down below continued.

Ethan pulled his leg out of the hole, imagining a tentacle reaching up to wrap around his ankle and pull him into the darkness. He screamed a thousand screams as he threw open the door and rushed out of this accursed house of the Devil.

Randy smacked him in the head with a very large branch and Ethan went to sleep for a while.

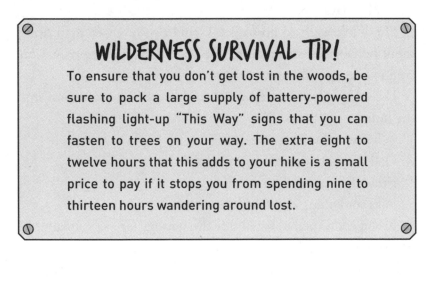

WILDERNESS SURVIVAL TIP!

To ensure that you don't get lost in the woods, be sure to pack a large supply of battery-powered flashing light-up "This Way" signs that you can fasten to trees on your way. The extra eight to twelve hours that this adds to your hike is a small price to pay if it stops you from spending nine to thirteen hours wandering around lost.

CHAPTER TWENTY-EIGHT

It was difficult to ignore all of the things that Erik was saying about Henry, none of which were even remotely flattering, but he had to focus on getting the gun before Mr. Grand did. If Henry had a gun and Mr. Grand did not, these next few minutes would go much more smoothly.

Mr. Grand was closer to the weapon, but Henry was…well, Henry couldn't think of any particular advantage he had. Youth maybe, though it wasn't like Mr. Grand was in his nineties. No, wait. Henry's advantage was that he desperately needed to redeem himself for shooting Erik with the arrow. If he saved his life, Erik's avalanche of profanity would eventually stop.

Henry was about nine or ten feet away from the gun and Mr. Grand was maybe six or seven. Henry could make up that distance if he pushed himself harder than he'd ever pushed himself before. Why didn't human beings come equipped with a turbo button?

An indeterminate percentage of a second later, he was six or seven feet away from the gun and Mr. Grand was three or four. But Henry might have gained an inch or two. Erik continued to point to the arrow in his arm and say unkind things about Henry's skills, intelligence, physical appearance, and family.

Mr. Grand was going to reach the gun first.

It was too late to turn around and pretend that he was uninvolved with whatever was going on here.

If Mr. Grand got the gun, Henry didn't think there was going to be a whole lot of diplomacy being practiced.

Mr. Grand's hand reached down for the weapon.

Henry dove for it.

Henry had not done a lot of diving in his life. In those rare occasions when he ventured into a swimming pool, he was purely a feetfirst kind of guy. He wouldn't even dive onto a Slip 'N Slide because he always worried it would be a good way to make his chest go *crunch*.

But he dove now. He leapt through the air, arms extended like Superman, trying to achieve more self-propelled forward momentum than he'd ever experienced.

He struck the ground. His chest thankfully did not go *crunch*. He did, however, immediately realize he should have started his dive about a second later because he was just lying on his stomach on the ground, not moving, with several inches between his fingertips and the gun.

Erik shouted something needlessly rude about his too-short dive.

Mr. Grand scooped up the gun.

Henry made another dive. Since he was lying on the ground, this dive did not have the same momentum as the previous one and was actually more of a lunge, but still, it propelled him forward those extra few inches so that Mr. Grand could stomp on his fingers.

It didn't feel good.

The weaker version of Henry would have just started screaming "Ow, ow, ow! My fingers! My precious fingers!" The new version of Henry screamed, of course. (After all, a man had just stomped on his fingers.) But he also leaned forward and bit Mr. Grand on the ankle, hard.

So hard, in fact, that Mr. Grand joined in the festival of screaming and dropped the gun.

The gun struck Henry on the head, which also did not feel good, but it gave him renewed hope that he would not be shot to death. He bit down even harder, trying to bite Mr. Grand's entire foot off even though he knew it was pretty unlikely that he'd be able to successfully do so.

Mr. Grand kicked Henry in the head with the foot that was currently not in the process of being bitten off, so Henry stopped biting.

The gun was right there, but fumbling around with the weapon was a good way to mess up his momentary advantage, so instead, Henry punched him in the knee, hoping that maybe Mr. Grand had recently had some sort of knee surgery or something.

In terms of places to punch somebody that won't make your knuckles feel like you've slammed them against a brick wall, the knee was not one of the better choices. And Mr. Grand's leg did not bend backward from the force of Henry's blow, which would have been nice. Still, he cried out in pain, and this gave Henry the self-confidence necessary to simply tackle the murderous cretin and knock him to the ground.

Mr. Grand wrapped his hands around Henry's neck.

Henry wrapped his hands around Mr. Grand's neck.

They stayed like that for a few moments, choking each other.

Henry understood that Erik had a lot to deal with right now, but a bit of help would be very much appreciated. Why not put that arrow in his arm to good use?

He was starting to feel a little dizzy. Mr. Grand was choking Henry harder than Henry was choking Mr. Grand.

Would pretending to be dead be useful? Probably not.

"Aaacck," said Henry.

"Guurgle," Mr. Grand replied.

Henry tried to bite Mr. Grand's fingers, but since they were wrapped tightly around his neck, Henry couldn't get access to them. He also tried to do the "smash your forehead into the forehead of your opponent" trick, but he couldn't move his head well enough.

It would be perfectly acceptable for Monica to come rescue him right about now.

Henry tried to suggest that they call a truce, though since it came out as "Aaacck" again, he didn't think Mr. Grand got his message.

His vision was going black.

* * *

Carnage-a-Plenty was not one of Henry's favorite video games and he'd probably played it for less than seventy-five or eighty hours total. But after each violence-filled level, your mentor, Splat-Tastic, would show up and give you words of wisdom to assist with the next level.

"*Two chainsaws are better than one.*"

"*When in doubt, use a flamethrower.*"

"*If facing an unbeatable enemy, do the unexpected.*"

Do the unexpected.

Henry imagined Splat-Tastic hovering above him on his magical carpet of dripping raw meat. "That is right, Henry. Do the unexpected."

"You mean give up? He wouldn't expect that."

Splat-Tastic rolled three of his four eyes. "No, Henry, I do not mean give up. I mean to do the unexpected."

"Like transform into a were-tiger, like on level eight?"

Splat-Tastic sighed and began to absentmindedly play with his exposed intestine. "No, first of all, you do not transform *into* a were-tiger. You *are* a were-tiger who transforms into a tiger. And we're talking about real life right now, not this undeniably great but not real video game, so you can't transform into a tiger."

"That's disappointing."

"Yeah, it is. But real life has better controls and more special moves than a video game."

"I love you, Splat-Tastic."

Splat-Tastic frowned. "Wow. The loss of oxygen is really getting to you. Time to make your unexpected move…fast! If you die, you can't just start over! Well, I mean, I'm not going to get into the potential for reincarnation or anything like that. I'm just a hallucination and don't have any insider knowledge of the afterlife. That said, I really do suggest that you figure out what kind of unexpected move you want to make and get around to making it before you lose consciousness. It's hard to defeat the bad guy when you're asleep."

"Any other advice?" Henry asked.

"No. What more could you possibly want?"

"Well, you have to admit, your advice was kind of vague."

"Oh, gee, gosh, excuse me for trying to help! I'm sorry that I can't give you some cheat code to get you through this, Mr. Ungrateful. I'm trying to give you the kind of help that lets you look within yourself for the true answer. But oh, no, you're all like 'Waaaah! I don't want to have to look within myself! I just want everything spelled out for me! Waaaah! Poor, superficial me!' You players are all alike. This is why I hate appearing as hallucinations. No appreciation."

"I'm sorry," said Henry. "I'm just a little stressed out right now. You know, because I'm being choked to death."

"Yeah, yeah, you guys are always offering 'I'm near death!' excuses for your rudeness. Well, that doesn't cut it with me. Go bite a donkey."

Splat-Tastic vanished into a puff of pixels.

"Nooooooo!" Henry bellowed. "Come back, Splat-Tastic! I need you, Splat-Tastic! You're my only friend!"

Do something unexpected—

* * *

Henry spat in Mr. Grand's face.

It wasn't a substantial loogie and the mucus-to-saliva ratio was not as gross as Henry would have preferred; however, Mr. Grand certainly wasn't expecting that.

Though he didn't recoil and go "Ew! Icky!" or anything like that, it did break his concentration for an instant, which was all that Henry needed to yank his neck free.

Then he did the "smash your forehead into the forehead of your opponent" trick. As a gigantic bolt of pain shot through his skull, he decided that it was a stupid trick that nobody should ever do.

Henry rolled off of Mr. Grand, wishing that his head didn't hurt quite so much. He was no doctor, but he was pretty sure that repeated head trauma was not the best way to avoid brain damage.

The gun. It was best not to forget about the gun.

He lunged for the gun just as Mr. Grand kicked it out of the way. Henry hoped that Erik would rush over and grab it, but then it occurred to him that Erik was no longer shouting horrible things about his ancestry. Erik lay on his back, breathing but not otherwise moving.

Bummer. Blood loss ruined everything.

Mr. Grand dove at Henry, doing a much better diving job than Henry had been able to accomplish. Henry got sort of smooshed into the ground, with Mr. Grand on top of him, but he managed to roll back over and throw a punch that missed.

"I'm going to tear your eyes out!" Mr. Grand shouted, clawing at Henry's eyes. He pinched some of Henry's eyelashes between his fingers and plucked them out.

Henry's reaction was not mild.

* * *

Monica stared at the unconscious man on the floor, wondering how he could remain unconscious like that when a bird was pecking away at his face. She thought perhaps she should shoo the bird away and then decided not to. She closed the door, giving them their privacy.

Randy emerged from the woods, holding a large branch.

"Did you find the other one?" Monica asked.

Randy nodded. "I've never seen that much fear in somebody's eyes. I guess we really scared him."

"What did you do to him?"

"Whacked him with a branch. He went down pretty easy. What about your guy?"

"Bird got him."

"Really?"

"Yeah."

"My bird?"

"I don't know what your bird looks like."

"Can I see it?"

"We should probably help Henry."

Henry screamed, sounding like somebody had ripped out some of his eyelashes.

Monica and Randy rushed off to help.

* * *

Mr. Grand reached for Henry's other eye. Henry slapped him away. "Stop it! Stop it! Stop it!"

"You're dead!" Mr. Grand snarled, even though "dead" was not an easy word to snarl.

Henry had to admit that he was getting tired of this. Who did this guy think he was, plucking out his eyelashes like that? There came a time when every man—and Henry felt that he qualified, if only barely—had to say, "Enough!"

Nobody attacked his friends and got away with it.

Nobody killed his insane counselor and got away with it.

And nobody—*nobody*—ripped out his eyelashes without getting punched in the face as hard as Henry could do it.

Henry threw the punch. Before it even connected with Mr. Grand's jaw, he thought, *Oh, yeah, this is gonna be a good one.*

And it was. It was not the mightiest punch ever thrown in the history of human punching, and if the recipient were a professional boxer instead of an exhausted criminal, the outcome would have been much different. But Henry's fist connected with a satisfying *smack* and Mr. Grand made a satisfying *uuggh*. And his head made a satisfying *boiiinnng* as it struck the ground, though that last one might have been in Henry's imagination.

He'd done it!

He'd delivered a final blow that had knocked his opponent unconscious! He'd defeated the evil Mr. Grand! He'd won the battle!

He quickly looked around for witnesses. Nobody had seen it.
Darn.

Oh, well. He still felt pretty good.

WILDERNESS SURVIVAL TIP!

If you're relying on this book for actual survival
tips, you're dead already.

CHAPTER TWENTY-NINE

Vincent "Foamer" Dansky, Glenn "Hatchet-Man" Thielbar, Quentin "Shredder" Hansen, and Karl "Die Die Die" Moore drove through the dirt road in a black van.

"We'd better get to kill some kids," said Foamer. "Last time we didn't. That maddened me." He cackled with laughter for no reason except that sometimes Foamer liked to cackle with laughter.

"Shut up," said Hatchet-Man. He was talking to Shredder, not Foamer. Hatchet-Man liked to tell people to shut up who weren't talking.

"I'm just saying I brought my best knife, and if I don't get to kill anybody with it, I'm going to be—"

"Shut up," said Hatchet-Man, this time talking to Foamer. "Mr. Grand said that the situation will probably be resolved before we get there. We're just emergency backup."

"Yeah, yeah, whatever." Foamer picked at his gums with one of his knives. "How much longer?"

Die Die Die, who was driving, didn't answer because he was distracted by the sight of a teenaged boy running across the road, maybe a hundred feet up ahead. He slammed on the brakes.

"I don't think it's resolved yet," he said.

The boy, a skinny little nerd, looked over at the van. He stood there, looking back and forth between the forest and the van, as if unsure whether to run from them or approach the vehicle.

Die Die Die opened the door and got out, hoping that the nerd couldn't see his tarantula tattoos from over there. "Hey, kid! You need any help?"

The nerd hesitated, still unsure, and then ran off into the woods.

"Hatchet-Man, Shredder…you two go after him. We'll keep driving to the destination."

Hatchet-Man nodded and slid open the side door of the van. He and Shredder got out and hurried down the road. "Hey, come back!" Hatchet-Man shouted. "We're not going to hurt—*yikes*!"

It was the only time in his life that Hatchet-Man had actually said the word "yikes." In any other circumstances, he would have been prepared for relentless teasing from his associates. However, right now he felt that they all understood how he was feeling, since there was a gigantic bear running down the road toward them.

Hatchet-Man and Shredder each fired off two ineffective shots and then ran back for the van, screaming. Die Die Die, who was not a man who placed great value in loyalty, had already put the van in reverse and was speeding away. But he couldn't get back around the corner without slowing down, so Hatchet-Man and Shredder were able to get back into the vehicle and slam the door closed.

"Forget this," said Die Die Die. "Grand didn't say anything about bears. He can deal with this himself. Everybody agree?"

Everybody except Hatchet-Man agreed, but he always liked to disagree just to cause conflict.

The reinforcements drove away.

* * *

"You're a terrible person," said Erik.

Henry nodded. "I know."

"You're the worst person I know and the worst person I've ever met, and if anybody tries to say that you're some kind of hero because of this, I'm going to set them straight," said Erik.

"Fair enough."

Mr. Grand, Ethan, and Chad were tied up and being held at gunpoint by Randy. Monica had done the actual tying of knots, so they didn't have to worry about any of them freeing themselves.

All three of the bad guys had cell phones, so they sent Jackie off in search of a signal. He'd come back half an hour later, saying that the police were on their way.

Henry did the best job he could on Erik's wound. He regained consciousness—angrily—after Henry applied the antiseptic and had remained in a foul mood ever since; however, it was clear that he wasn't going to bleed to death and Henry felt that he could eventually convince him that girls were really into guys who'd been shot through the arm with arrows.

Stu returned to camp, out of breath, and hid in the barracks until the others were able to convince him that if a bear *had* been following him, it at least was not doing so any longer.

"Nice job," Monica told Henry. "Not all of it, but most of it. I'm impressed."

"Thanks," he said.

They sat in silence for a moment. Henry felt that this was the opportunity to say something important…but could he handle the rejection?

Sure. Why not? He almost got killed today, so having his heart crushed would be nothing.

"So, Monica…?"

"Yes?"

"Do you want to…do something…sometime?"

"Are you asking me out?"

"Yeah. I mean, not if you already have a boyfriend. I'm not trying to horn in on Bobby's action or anything."

"Bobby?"

"Bobby. I saw the text where he…uh, said he misses your… misses you. Is he your boyfriend?"

"No."

"Seriously?"

"Ex-boyfriend. He's having trouble with the 'ex' part. But we're not together."

"Is this something that you're heartbroken over?"

"Not anymore."

"So did you want to do something sometime?"

"You know that we live in different cities, right?"

"Yeah."

"And that you're not my usual type?"

"I figured."

"And that you've caused me a huge amount of trouble since we met, including but not limited to an injured shoulder and people trying to kill me?"

"If you go out with me, I promise that nobody will try to kill you on our first date," said Henry, hoping he wasn't lying when he said that.

"That's very romantic."

"Thanks."

"How about we just kiss and take it from there?"

"I am completely okay with that."

They kissed.

Then they smiled at each other and kissed again and the

fireworks in Henry's mind were so vivid and glorious that they drowned out the sound of Erik repeatedly telling him he was a complete jerk.

SPECIAL ADDENDUM TO THE NEW BOOK VERSION OF THE MOVIE VERSION OF THE BOOK

Henry sits in the theater, large popcorn in his lap, Monica to his left, Randy to his right. Stu, Jackie (now purple-haired), and Erik (who has almost but not quite gotten over his rage) also sit in the row with him. Henry's parents are in the theater, but they sit a few rows back so as not to cramp his sweet style.

"We need to work together," says Henry, though this is the Henry on-screen and not the real Henry. He has a low, gravelly voice and is played by a twenty-three year-old actor. On-screen Henry tosses machine guns to the Hollywood counterparts of Randy, Jackie, Monica, and Peter. (Erik and Stu have been combined into one character for the movie.) "We're not going to let them push us around anymore! We've all been saying that we have a bad feeling about this and I agree. We have a bad feeling about this…because of what's going to happen to *them*!"

Everybody raises their machine guns in unison.

"They killed Max and they killed Frank. And they killed Hector, and yes, they even killed Old Mr. Winkerston. But they aren't going to kill us!"

A gunshot rings out. Peter clutches at his chest, gives a heart-rending six-minute soliloquy that will get him nominated for a People's Choice Award, and then dies.

Mr. Grand, Ethan, Chad, and the thirteen other assassins leap out of the forest, their own machine guns blasting. Seventeen minutes of nonstop action follow, with computer-generated blood spraying everywhere.

Monica (the real one) snuggles closer to Henry as the on-screen Henry throws a boomerang at Ethan. Ethan drops to the ground, neck broken, as the boomerang returns to Henry's hand.

There are lots of explosions.

Henry leaps onto a motorcycle and starts the engine. Monica leaps on behind him, facing backward so that she can take out more assassins with her machete. As they race down the dirt road, the assassins on their own motorcycles drive up beside them, swinging maces and wrenches at them, but they are no match for Monica's machete.

Henry spins the motorcycle around, tires squealing, and then races back toward camp.

"What are you doing?" asks Monica. "Safety is in the other direction!"

"There can be no safety while those madmen still live," Henry tells her. The real Henry doesn't think that they'd be able to hear each other that well over the roar of a motorcycle motor, but that's no big deal. This is the movies.

As Henry speeds down the road, he is joined by Randy and Jackie, also on motorcycles. (How they got behind him is not entirely clear. Henry hopes that after the premiere, they'll tighten some of the editing.)

Mr. Grand and his few remaining assassins are also on motorcycles, speeding right toward them!

Movie Henry slams his fist down on the turbo button, and his motorcycle shoots forward. Real Henry likes to believe that had motorcycles been available to him at that particular time, he would have done the same thing.

In super-slow motion, Henry's motorcycle collides with Mr. Grand's. Yes, it is somewhat reckless of Henry to do this when he has a passenger, but no doubt Monica can handle herself in a 120-mile-per-hour head-on motorcycle collision.

The three of them are catapulted into the air by the force of the crash. The motorcycles explode beneath them.

Henry thinks it would be seriously cool if the movie counterparts had an extended fight sequence on the way down, but that isn't the kind of reality-based entertainment this motion picture was about. They hit the ground first and *then* begin their extended fight sequence.

"You killed my mentor," Henry growls. "But you won't kill anybody else!" He punches Mr. Grand in the face three times, a bucket of blood splashing with each blow.

Randy leans over to Henry and whispers "I thought this was supposed to be PG-13?"

"What are you talking about?" Henry whispers back. "This has had the F-word about two thousand times."

"Oh, yeah. Sorry."

They go back to watching the movie. In the exciting finale, Henry and Mr. Grand battle each other with their bare hands, delivering more punishment than anybody who isn't a character in an action movie could possibly take until Henry finally grabs Mr. Grand's nose and gives it a devastating twist.

"Hey, that's a bunch of garbage!" Jackie says, standing up. "I'm the one who did that!" His mom tugs him back down into his seat.

Henry gives Mr. Grand's nose one final twist and it comes off. Mr. Grand howls in pain, dousing Henry in red, and finally drops to the ground, dead.

Monica throws her arms around Henry, clearly not worried about getting bloodstains all over her clothes.

"I don't know about you," says Henry, "but I have a good feeling about this."

"I do too," says Monica. "A very good feeling."

They kiss.

On the movie screen, the picture fades to black, followed by these words: *Dedicated to the memory of Max. You were the wind beneath our wings.*

As the lights come up and the audience gives a standing ovation, Henry puts his arms around Monica and kisses her like the action hero he always knew he could be.

* * *

Henry stands in front of thirty campers. "Okay, everybody, welcome to Strongwoods Survival Camp, under new ownership. If you've seen the movie, you saw what it did for me. And now I'm going to do the same for you!"

"That's right," says Randy, wearing a camouflage shirt. "Don't think this is going to be an easy two weeks for you. We will test your skills like they've never been tested before!"

"But it will be fun too," says Monica, also wearing a camouflage shirt. "Before we begin, are there any questions?"

One of the campers raises his hand. "Does this camp have an arcade?"

Henry, Randy, and Monica exchange a weary look. This is going to be a long two weeks.

THE END

ABOUT THE AUTHOR

In a true wilderness survival situation, Jeff Strand would last maybe fifteen minutes—half an hour tops—though he is proud to say that he wouldn't be all whiny while he died. His previous novel for young adults was *A Bad Day for Voodoo*, which was called "The greatest book ever written in the entire history of human existence," by somebody, somewhere, hopefully. Those who said that *Voodoo* was "really, really, really stupid," are likely to say the exact same thing about *I Have a Bad Feeling About This*. Jeff Strand lives in Tampa, Florida (about an hour from Disney World!). You can e-mail him at JeffStrand@aol.com and visit his glorious website at www.JeffStrand.com.

A BAD DAY FOR VOODOO

Jeff Strand

When your best friend is just a tiny bit psychotic, you should never actually believe him when he says, "Trust me. This is gonna be awesome."

Of course, you probably wouldn't believe a voodoo doll could work either. Or that it could cause someone's leg to blow clean off with one quick prick. But I've seen it. It can happen.

And when there's suddenly a doll of YOU floating around out there—a doll that could be snatched by a Rottweiler and torn to shreds, or a gang of thugs ready to torch it, or any random family of cannibals (really, do you need the danger here spelled out for you?)—well, you know that's just gonna be a really bad day…

PRAISE FOR *A BAD DAY FOR VOODOO*:

"For a reader intentionally seeking a wacky horror/comedy,
this book delivers." —*VOYA*

"Jeff Strand is the funniest writer in the game, and *A Bad Day for Voodoo*
is wicked, wicked fun. Dark, devious and delicious!" —Jonathan Maberry,
New York Times bestselling author of *Rot & Ruin* and *Flesh & Bone*

STUPID FAST
Geoff Herbach

I AM NOT STUPID FUNNY. I AM STUPID FAST.

My name is Felton Reinstein, which is not a fast name. But last November, my voice finally dropped and I grew all this hair and then I got stupid fast. Fast like a donkey. Zing!

Now they want me, the guy they used to call Squirrel Nut, to try out for the football team. With the jocks. But will that fix my mom? Make my brother stop dressing like a pirate? Most important, will it get me girls—especially Aleah?

So I train. And I run. And I sneak off to Aleah's house in the night. But deep down I know I can't run forever. And I wonder what will happen when I finally have to stop.

PRAISE FOR GEOFF HERBACH:

"In the tradition of Holden Caulfield and Eric 'Moby' Calhoune comes Felton Reinstein." —*VOYA*

"Deep, moving, LOL funny and completely original."
—*School Library Journal*